ISBN 978-0-244-76589-7

Cover artwork by: the author

CHAPTERS

"...For ours is not a conflict against mere flesh and blood,

but against the despotisms, the empires, the forces and authorities

that control and govern all of the darkness

of this age in the world

- against all of the spiritual hosts of evil

arrayed against us in this heavenly warfare..."

Ephesians 6:12

CHAPTER 1

Lunch At The Harbour

She glanced down at her watch, good, most of the lunch hour remained despite being delayed in getting away from the confines of the small but busy Estate Agents office, where she worked in the town centre of the seaside resort of Scarborough, in the North East of England. There was still plenty of time left to enjoy some warm sunshine, and have fresh sea air to breathe, under a bright blue summer sky. This Monday morning had been even busier than it normally was so the time had passed quickly, but it had been tiring nonetheless – mainly because last night she'd had a lot less sleep than usual.

So she was really looking forward now to having some quiet and restful time to herself, with just her thoughts about last night for company. Plenty of time now after a brisk walk weaving through and across the ever crowded pedestrian precinct, then taking the short-cut down a long, perpetually shaded narrow alley with its steep and very old, well worn stone steps. The alley was squeezed inbetween the rows of tall Victorian brick built properties, now converted into shops and flats. The steep steps slowed her pace down, but the alley was a much quicker route, as it lead straight down to the harbour.

Emerging from the dimmer light of the narrow alleyway, back again into the bright sunshine, she looked over to the far end of the harbour wall and was pleased to see that one of her favourite benches was unoccupied, even though there were lots of holiday makers milling around. It was a favourite because it looked over the whole bay as well as the harbour and the steep cliffs with the ancient castle ruins on top of them. Resuming her brisk pace she quickly made her way over to it. Right - a bit of of 'me-time' now she thought, sitting down and putting her shoulder bag next to her and taking her lunch box out of it. Here she was well away from all the constant distractions at work, so she could now replay in her mind what she'd experienced last night.

She'd listened intently and learned *such a lot* last night. What she'd listened to and learned about from the man who'd given a talk in the old marquee at the Scarborough Fair had started to change, well, everything for her.   Yeah…that's not exaggerating, *just about everything,* she thought.   Because since she'd left the Fair and then later laid awake in her bed thinking about it all into the early hours, unable to sleep, she had been seeing and thinking about everything very – no, not very - *completely* - differently from the old perceptions of the world around her that she used to have…before. And it was just from pure chance or coincidence and sheer curiosity she supposed, that she'd walked into that old marquee, sited in a far corner, to listen to the man's talk and presentation *just as he was starting!*

As she'd sat listening to him talk, talk - yes, but what he did was much more than that. It was obvious from the start that he was a very gifted and experienced orator. The way he could *really communicate* a clear understanding of what at first would seem to be really complex things, had really grabbed her attention.   He'd begun by fairly quickly covering lots of interesting, different but loosely connected subjects, but all to do with how we see and perceive things that happen in our lives. He'd then slowly brought them altogether towards the end of the hour or so, and the result for her had been, well, there's no other way to put it, a revelation, an epiphany. Because during that hour or so it had gradually dawned on her that her previously held perceptions and beliefs – oh yeah, that's how he'd put it - he'd said; *'what you perceive – leads you to what you believe...!'* - about human life and the world we all live in - were so *obviously* programmed to be false and very limited...And so they had been – and it felt like they still were being - massively updated, renewed...changed.

On a canal barge holiday with her parents, years ago, she remembered watching a sluice gate being slowly raised up so the river that had been held back by it was freed to begin to - more and more powerfully - surge through it - and go beyond...raising their boat and enabling them to proceed with their journey. She felt that what she was going through now, since last night, was just like that scene...

She felt as well that listening to him last night had also kick-started the process of her waking up to a new dawn after a deep, long sleep. Or of being somehow de-tranced, after her twenty something years so far, and realising that she must've been, well, like *sleep walking* for so many years before! Kinda like in a trance. But now, at last, she was waking up, opening her eyes and becoming open and receptive to perceive – and believe - so much more now that was, well, new and exciting!

Her initial perception shifts had been gradual at first, but like that river, they had quickly gained pace, and later in bed, her mind still racing in the early hours of this morning, she'd compared it as well to a very recent 'travelling experience' when she'd been a passenger - a pillion rider on a motorbike for the very first time! At the end of the long trip, when she'd finally gotten off the bike, her legs all wobbly and her tummy a little bit travel sick, she'd struggled but eventually managed to suss out the fiddly and unwilling-to-open locking strap, and then finally taken off the 'so-heavy-it-droops-your-head-down' full face motorbike helmet. A helmet that had a very narrow, dim, dirty and scratched visor that she could only blurringly see through, and which also blocked most of her hearing out.

So she hadn't been able to see very much at all of the views over the lovely North Yorkshire Moors that abounded the coastal road to Whitby, before turning off to visit the picturesque village of Goathland where the T.V. period drama series 'Heartbeat', set in the 1960s, had been mostly filmed. Taking that helmet off had been a joy when they'd got there because she could then see and hear properly again - and she didn't feel like her head was trapped in a tight cage any longer!

She'd thought it'd been a pretty good comparison as far as it went, because the thing was - was that before last night's listening, learning, and starting to wake up, she hadn't really been aware that up until then she'd actually, *metaphorically speaking,* had a perception and sense restricting, cage-like-helmet like that one on! - Let alone that it had a quick release strap on it! - Even if she had known she'd been wearing one!

I suppose, as the years went by, you just got used to accepting and resigning yourself to the way things were, her thoughts continued, familiarity an'all that...it's just the way they are...just the way life is...After all don't most folk live, no, couldn't call it living, it's just *existing* - like they're driving a 'dodgem car'? - You pootle along, year in year out, round and round a set and predictable circuit, with occasional or regular collisions that you never saw coming, or if you did see them coming you thought there was nothing you could do to avoid them? Then, eventually, when the ride's over for you, when your time's up, the power gets switched off, so out you climb, and away you go? *So what's that all about...?!*

Ever since you waved goodbye to your childhood you've tried to answer that perennial question: *'what's it all about?!'* She grinned then as the opening bars to the theme tune of the '60s film: *'What's It All About – Alfie?'* sung by Cilla Black suddenly played in her mind – because you've always wanted to be able to do more with your life than just ride it like a dodgem car - whilst unknowingly wearing that sense stunting helmet, but then, because your 'rational' world-view-as-it-appears-to-you system programmed left brain's perception had grown in its dominance over you, as a *response* – but in no way an *answer* to that question - it always came back with, *'well...that's all very well – but this is the 'real' world dude,* this is what's *normal!* So c'mon - *let's be rational* about this - it just is, always was...and always will be for you...! *So just accept it, stop moaning about it and get on with it...!'*

And what was it the man had said about *'being rational'* last night? - Oh yeah, that was it - he'd said: 'just be aware – and beware – that at the end of the road of 'Rationality'...*lies the stillness, and silence, of the mass grave...!'*

Wow! That had been – and still was! - a deep – and scary image he'd verbally conjured up...! That'd really shook me up big time and made me think!

But...even so, during all those years since childhood, even though you'd more or less 'had to' fully resign yourself and comply with it all, deep down inside of you, in your inner heart of hearts, you'd always kinda sensed, vaguely, that, well, that there's something you've forgotten. Something you've lost. Something huge *you think you once knew*, long, long ago, and you used 'it' naturally to really live, not just exist. But now it seems you've forgotten 'it', or else 'it' must've been, somehow taken away from you, long, long ago. And the world and its whole system, the way it seems to work, and all the things going on in it happening all around you that just don't make any sense - and there's more and more of them happening these days, from tedious, irritating and unnecessary bureaucratic intrusive controls into your life, to the really horrific things shown to be happening all over the world in the constant

'News' on the television. They're all just...just, well, *they're just not 'right'!* And especially not right to that faint trace you still have of a deep, old, ever fleeting and vague memory, of another way of living - living with a sense of fulfilment, happiness, joy, and with, yes, of course, with challenges, but well, with the exhilaration those *naturally occurring* challenges gave you...

But...then...one day...*something just happens...!* and you take that heavy, perception and sense dimming, restricting cage-like-helmet off, and let all the true light shine in, and then you find that you can raise your head and see all the magnificent views to incredibly far distant horizons. Views, landscapes and horizons that you obviously just hadn't seen, known about, or had any perception of before – so you couldn't even *start to believe* they actually, really existed! But actually, and really, they did – and they had been all around you all of the time! Instead you had just been seeing – perceiving - a narrow, short range, dim and dusty view of a diminished world that was only right in front of you, whilst you were going round and round in circles on the dodgem track...

Now I can also not only really see, but also hear everything better, clearer, and...and...*oh - everything else...!...Because it's not just what I can see and hear either!* – with my normal five senses - what I can see, hear, touch, taste, and smell, that all seem so much more intense now! *Because the really, really big thing is – is that there's these other, just as 'real' senses that I've obviously got because I'm really becoming aware of them as being a natural part of me as well now - but I never knew about them before! They're still slightly kinda in the background yet, but I know they're steadily getting closer...*

- Something like that anyway! She thought, taking another bite of her cheese and pickles sandwich.

And that's something else as well! - She nodded to herself, chewing slowly - the way I'm now starting *to...really...enjoy...thinking!* Engaging my right brain - and more besides - which those 'new senses' seem to have something to do with, it all really does seem almost effortless now, and it's a real, natural pleasure to do it! – Not just *have to do it,* like I used to when forced to confront and solve some perceived problems – that was like being stuck in first gear, with 'my engine' revving into the red line, and getting me all hot and bothered! My thinking *now* seems to have suddenly become 'unstuck' and gone up way more than just a gear or three! So it's all just so much faster, easier, calmer, clearer, sharper – bigger and better!

Guess it was definitely true what the man at the Fair had said towards the end of his talk:

'As your consciousness expands, your whole system of thinking will change...'

She grinned widely as she thought that it's like having a new head, well, not a new one exactly, it's still my old one but it's been upgraded, serviced, tuned up and is now at last firing on all cylinders! But...I also get the feeling, *the sense*, the thought, that there are *still* lots more cylinders to fire up, there's a lot more potential, a lot more power, and, in time, when I'm running on all of them, I'll be ready, I'll set out on another journey to where I'm going, and do what I came here for...*Huh!? Where did that thought come from?!* She questioned herself, a bemused grin on her face.

So all in all, *it...really...is...incredible!* she mused, and grinning widely now, she raised her head and looked up into the deep summery blue sky, really seeing it as if for the first time, and marvelled that she was now so aware that the warm blue sky just went on and on, and on...and a big part of her, which she thought must be one of those 'new' senses, way down deep inside of her, irresistibly wanted to reach up and out, to soar up into it, and become at one with it for a while....and she gasped out a loud, ecstatic... *"WOWwwwwwwww!"*

"Errr - *giv' y'a penny for 'em Sophie?!"* A familiar, and friendly, deep masculine voice interrupted her sudden reverie, causing her to immediately return to the here and now.

"OHHH! *Oh Hi Jake!* Sorry...I, I was miles away...*nearly!"* She giggled.

"Oh – No – *I'm Sorry…! Don't want to intrude on y'avin yer lunch like!* But I saw y'sat over 'ere – an' then I 'eard y'*'Wowww-in!'* - Reckon most folk 'ere in the 'arbour did an'all!' - An' so I just couldn't help meself! I 'ad a feelin' like to 'ave a ride out an' just cum down 'ere today, now, for a change, to 'ave a stroll around the 'arbour, get some fresh air, an' it gets me out the workshop shed fer a bit – nice coincidence I saw you 'ere too! So, anyway, I thought I'd come over and say 'ello!"

"Oh that's okay...glad you did! Just daydreaming...I guess...thinking about last night – so, how you doing?!"

"Yeah, doin' good ta, er - *last night*?! – Oh? - *Oh!* - You went to Fair - *didn't you?*"

"Yeah, I did - hey – thought you were going as well with all the lads from the bike club...boys' night out?! I asked one of them if you were there as well, but he hadn't seen you..."

"Aye he called round this mornin' wi some bike bits for me an' he told me you did. *I was goin'*, it was a pity but summat else bloomin' cropped up wi' a job I'm on, right at last minute - still on wi' it now - an' I got carried away, kept on at it 'til late, wantin' to get it sorted, but I didn't – I'm still tryin' to! Might go tonight though...er, I, er, don't s'ppose y'd fancy goin' again would you, a second visit like..?"

"Well, yeah...yeah 'course I would! There was something,

and someone I'd like to see again actually, and...well, and I think you'd be blown over by it and him as well Jake!"

"Oh, right... er, nice one! Thanks! Well, 'ows about I cum round on t'bike, pick y'up about seven – an' don't worry about goin' on't bike - I'll bring y'a *new spare 'elmet!* Weather's great for a ride an'all.."

"Yeah seven'd be great – what? – You've gotta *new* spare helmet?"

"Aye! Well...after I borrowed me mate's spare one last time for y'when we'ad that ride out to Goathland, I sort o', well, bought one y'could use next time, er, *'opin' there'd be a next time like*...this time...it's a lightweight open face one. I know y'didn't like the heavy full face one, as y'said after, er...what was it…? Made me laugh - Oh aye! - y'said: *'it was obviously owned by some smelly, greasy biker...who must be a danger on't roads as y'can't 'ardly see owt through it...!'"* He said chuckling at the memory.

Sophie laughed, and said, "Ohh that's really sweet of you

Jake, oh thank you! Aaah! – But hey! *Please don't tell him I said all that about it – and him!"*

"Uuuh, it's too late, I sorta hinted that to 'im...! But don't worry – Simmo's thick skinned – he's gotta hide like a rhino...!" He grinned.

"*Ooops!* Still...it was nothing a week of intense shampooing and conditioning didn't sort out!" She said with mock seriousness, a mischievous glint in her eyes.

"What! Eh! *Oh no*! Really...?"

"Joking...!

"Oh...Yeah! Ha! Er, so, well, I'll er, I'll see y'...'bout seven then..?"
"Yes, that's great, I'll look forward to it, thanks, Jake.."

"Right then...great! Well, s'ppose I'll 'ave t'get back – still got that engine for the new chopper I'm makin' - an' I've bin workin' on 'til daft o'clock for days now - all in bits – again!

But I'll knock off now at six, get cleaned up an' come round for you at seven. - Laters then Sophie!"

"Yeah! Laters Jake!" With a happy smile on her face she watched him stride away until she soon lost sight of his tall figure wearing a black leather waistcoat with the motorcycle club's back patch he'd sewn on to it, as he merged into the crowds of holiday makers and sight seers near the harbour entrance. She soon heard the roar of his bike as he fired it up and rode away.

Well...I didn't expect that! She thought. Maybe it's one of those coincidences the man at the Fair was talking about, and a nice one as well! Maybe it's intended I go back...and with Jake...Mmm, I'm looking forward to it! It'll get me through this afternoon's dreary workload.

And so, light-heartedly and with a nice feeling of anticipation, she finished her sandwich lunch, basking in the warm sunshine at the picturesque harbour, whilst thinking her thoughts and people watching the milling tourist crowds.

She then wandered upto Scarborough's old town Market

20

Vaults to do some window shopping amongst all the intriguing little shops and stalls there, before going back to the office. Then she was sat at her desk for the afternoon, for more of the same old, same old at the Estate Agents.

CHAPTER 2

Scarborough Fair

J ake parked his custom chopped motorbike up in the field being used as a car park next to the Fair. Sophie dismounted and with feline grace she stretched her arms up high, arching her back, and then took off her new light weight shiny white open face helmet and retro style goggles. She pulled and shook her long, raven black hair loose out from under her burgundy coloured leather jacket, so it all spilled down her back, and finger combed through the glossy locks.

"Wowww! That waaasss grrreat!" She beamed at him.

"And this helmet you got for me is great too! It made it all so much better than that first time! I *really enjoyed* this ride! Ha ha! – I'm starting to see now why you love riding bikes so much! Think I'm getting the bug too!" She laughed.

"Well, I took it right steady like, as it's only y'second time, that first time y'were really tense." Jake hadn't minded that at all really, because she had clung onto him so tightly.

"Yeah, I know, I was...but I really get it now - it's like low level flying, and soaring free like a bird - just passing by everything and all those slow plodding cars! You're such a good rider, I feel really safe with you and trust you...I..." She realised she was gushing, but didn't care! – It was probably due to the thrill, exhilaration and speed of the ride, she thought, which hadn't seemed 'steady' at all to her! – She'd never moved so fast in her life! And this time because she hadn't had a sight restricting cage on her head she had clearly seen all the scenery whiz past them! Then, as they had got closer to the Fair, there had been a few times when she'd quickly closed her eyes though, as Jake skilfully weaved and filtered the bike quickly and closely through all the slow and queuing traffic - that had been exciting!

Then with a girlish hip jiggle in her tight blue jeans she said, full of excitement, *"C'mon, c'mon! Let's go see the Fair!"*

Jake grinned and chained up the big powerful black and

chrome motorbike to a sturdy metal fence post, and put their helmets carefully together in a brown leather and canvas shoulder bag he'd made, so he could easily carry both of them hands free.

They walked the short distance over the grass field to the Fair, the slowly setting late summer sun cast multi hued streaks of reddish orange glows over the sky, and the Fair's myriad bright multi coloured lights awaiting them twinkled in a surreal kaleidoscope of colours. The loud music of popular tunes mixed in a raucous medley with the many different snatches of sounds that floated over enticingly to them, and then, as they wandered into the stalls the exciting atmosphere and all the sounds and lights washed over them like waves.

The Scarborough Fair was no small affair this year, it must've covered an area the size of 4 or 5 football pitches, sited on farm land a few miles from the town, and it wasn't just one Fair this year but three travelling Fairs that had all come together, and joined forces for the first time ever, offering a week of entertainment, the biggest Scarborough Fair ever! Even though it was still fairly early in the evening the walkways were almost packed with people enjoying themselves.

Sophie slipped her hand under Jake's big black leather jacketed arm and smiled up at him, cutely wrinkling her nose, suddenly realising just how much she really did like this big Baloo of a man. Yes, she thought, that's who he'd always reminded her of, that huge bear in the Jungle Book, that sounds silly I know, she thought to herself, but I really do feel at ease and happy when I'm with him. She scrunched her shoulders together as she squeeze hugged his arm even tighter for a moment and smiled up at him again, and Jake's broad shining smile immediately flashed brightly down at her, silently telling her that he too felt...

"Ooh! Look Jake! - That wasn't here last night! *Let's go see...!"* Sophie exclaimed.

Just off to the side of them was an old fashioned genuine looking Romany gypsy caravan, with a large, very ornately hand painted sign standing in front of it stating that Gypsy Magda Leah Rose would tell you all about your fortune, your future lovelife - and a host of other things that were all detailed on it – that you needed to know were in your future!

"Wow! That caravan is a classic...*amazin' job!"* Jake said, standing still to admire it. Sophie was tugging at his arm to pull him towards it, "Ok! Ok! *I'm cumin', I'm cumin'!"* He laughed. They squeezed through to the front of a small crowd milling around the caravan. As soon as they got within a few yards of the wooden steps that lead up into it, a multi coloured tapestried curtain covering its doorway swished open and what appeared to be a very old lady then quite agilely stepped down the wooden steps to the ground. Her eyes had gazed directly at Sophie and Jake from the moment she had pulled the curtain to one side and popped her head out - it was as if she had been expecting them right at that very moment Sophie thought!

"Hello My Dears!" The old gypsy lady said to them.

Her voice wasn't loud, but as all the other sounds around them had suddenly seemed to recede they could both hear her quite clearly, *"I knew you would come you see, and I'm so pleased you're both here at last..."*
Her voice was very much at odds with her appearance,

because it belonged to a much younger woman, and she had an unusual accent that Sophie couldn't place. And her eyes, Sophie had never seen such deeply twinkling emerald green eyes, they were so bright and young looking, but so old and ancient wisdom filled at the same time, and framed by very long, natural looking reddish auburn hair, without a streak of grey in it, that reached freely down to her waist.

"Oh!... Wow! Er..." Sophie exclaimed, taken aback, and she rapidly looked up to Jake, then back to the lady.

By now the old gypsy lady who had seemed to almost glide over the grass in her long flowing purple and green long sleeved dress stood closely in front of Jake and Sophie, and she reached out to gently touch Jake's hand, as stared into his eyes and said, "there is so much for you to know that we have to tell you, young man....Jake." Then still holding Jake's hand she gently touched Sophie's hand and turning her head she looked deeply into Sophie's eyes, "...and for you my dear Sophie, there are many more things we can tell you – to help you - to add to what you now...have already started to know...again."

"Oh!?   W,what d'you mean?   How d'you know our..!?" Sophie burbled.

With a radiant smile that lit up her face the gypsy lady raised her palm and hushed Sophie.

"What a handsome couple you both make, you remind me so much of..."

Her voice wavered, and she seemed to stare right through them both for a moment, before shaking her head causing her long hair to shimmer and float around her.

"But I've just been asked not to delay you too much now, as there is someone else who needs to see you both...so will you then come back and see me later my dears…?"

"Er, y,yes, okay...I guess so, we, er, we could do that couldn't we Soph..?" Jake asked looking intently at Sophie.

"Yeess," she replied slowly.

"So, er, ok, we'll see you later then, er, M,Magda Leah Rose...?" Jake said.

"*Wonderful!* We will meet again later...afterwards, and you'll both understand much more by then as well, and how...I can help you, but in the meantime...please, I must say, just be aware, and please just be careful, there are some others here tonight, that, well, they are not like you, because...they, well, they're not really from here.."

She looked fixedly at Jake for a moment before continuing, "Soon you too will have much to do young man Jake, but you are true and strong and far more powerful than you could ever think you are at this moment in time, and, with all our help, you will be better able to protect both of you, and perhaps...oh I do so hope, this time, perhaps..." She then looked around her, "*...all of these and so many other other souls as well...*"

She said that last part almost to herself, looking around at the multitude of people eddying by all around them. "*So...!* Well then, take care my dears - and I'll see you both soon!"

By the time either Sophie or Jake had gathered their wits enough to reply to these quite unexpected and slightly disconcerting parting comments, the old gypsy lady was nearly at the top of the steps and back inside her caravan.

"Er, sorry, but, who, who wants, er, to see us, what are..?!" Sophie called out to her.

Gypsy Magda Leah Rose paused, and turning her head she smiled beatifically at them both, her glinting emerald like eyes fixed on them. She then seemed to tense herself as if deeply concentrating for a few seconds, and both Sophie and Jake felt a sudden feeling of caressing warmth and light that seemed to emanate from her and envelop them.

"You will soon see, my dears..."

And with that she disappeared into the caravan, the colourful heavy curtain swishing closed.

All the sounds around them suddenly came back, just as loud as they had been before they briefly met the strange old lady called Gypsy Magda Leah Rose. They both just stood there, still and mute, staring at the caravan's doorway. Jake was the first to recover, "OH...Wowww, that, er, she, *was somethin' else!*" He said blowing out his breath and shaking his head.

"An' 'ow did she know our names?! I've 'eard some bloomin' good sales pitches in me time but..."

"I don't think that was a sales pitch Jake", Sophie quietly interrupted him, as she continued staring at the colourful curtain covering the caravan's doorway. "I think, I think it was like, like she was giving us a preview of the good news, the nice news first, then a warning, sort of, of the bad news".

"Huh!?"

"Oh, *I dunno!* But I did get a good feeling from...about her! C'mon Jake, let's go around, and then I really want to go again and show you where I went last night...see the man again I listened to, and then we'll come back here and see her later...is that ok?"

31

"Yeah. Okay...Aye! No probs...*But...Beware...there's some 'ere not really from 'ere...!*" He mimicked mockingly, but in a deep humorously slow solemn voice the words that the old gypsy lady had said to them. Sophie playfully and lightly slap punched him on his upper arm.

"Don't mock! *You never know!*" She said, then looked around her exaggeratedly, her pale blue eyes over widely vigilant before quickly looking back into his, a barely restrained smile on her lips. She then stepped back in amusement and watched him rubbing his arm where she had very lightly punch slapped him moments before, his face now grimaced in an expression of over acted pain.

"Aaah! You big baby! Did that hurt?!" She pouted at him, stepping back with her hands on her hips, joining in with his horse playing. "No it didn't!" She answered for him, then said - "But this...will..!!" As she playfully drew her hand back pretending to punch slap him again, but Jake quickly moved his hands up to shoulder height in mock surrender, "I give in, I give in, *you win!*" He pantomime wailed.

"Tee Hee!...Knew I would!" She giggled as she skipped back to his side to clutch his arm, looked up into his face and burst out laughing with him at the same time as he did, and they then walked away leaning closely together, still laughing.

But...unseen by them, close-by, hidden in plain sight amongst all the people meandering around, the black malevolent eyes of a middle aged nondescript man narrowed as he watched Sophie and Jake mingle back into the crowds, before he started to follow them...

Sophie and Jake slowly wandered off, relaxed and increasingly happy in each others company, but still moving purposefully in the general direction of the far corner of the Fair that Sophie wanted to visit again.

Unaware that all the while they were being stalked...

They stopped occasionally, pleasantly distracted, to watch and enjoy some of the attractions, and Jake was delighted when they came across an archery range, where he won a garish multi coloured carnival glass vase for hitting the gold bulls eye with all six of his arrows. Sophie clapped excitedly and hopped lightly up and down with both feet as the sixth arrow flew unerringly in amongst all the others, and she was really genuinely touched when he presented his prize to her, bowing with a pantomimed chivalric flourish, saying that he promised to get her some flowers tomorrow to put in it. Praising his skill with the bow she was amazed when he admitted that he was a member of the Scarborough Archers and practised at the club at least a couple of times a week, and maybe, just maybe, he might be entering the County's English Long Bow Championships later in the autumn.

As they continued strolling and chatting away together, Sophie could now sense more and more of the many hidden, inner depths to this big and outwardly almost shy man. Depths that she hadn't been even remotely aware of before, after their first, well, 'date-on-two-wheels', really. But, she thought, that's because it was *'before'* - when I was using my *'old head'! But now...!*

The cold and feral eyes of the nondescript man stalking them had watched every move they'd made, and he moved closer behind them to try and overhear what they were saying.

They eventually arrived in the general area that Sophie had been aiming them towards, here in the far corner of the Fairground. She stopped walking and letting go of Jake's arm she turned in a full circle, hugging the glass vase to her chest with both hands as she looked around her. As she looked back to where they had just walked from she couldn't help but notice a middle aged man, just a few yards behind them, abruptly change direction and almost furtively scamper away down a shadowy alleyway where the large trucks and muffled generators powering the nearby stalls and rides were parked. With so many people moving about in all directions all around her she only registered the man's movement fleetingly, and it would only be later that she realised its significance...

"S'funny." She said disappointedly. "*It's changed.* It's not the same as last night! *It's not here!* Where is it...?"

"- Er, well, mebbe it's like Tescoes – when they keep movin' things around, just when y'get used to where they all are, so y'ave to spend more time in there 'cause then they hope y'll spend more money?!" Jake said, not entirely sure what she was looking for, as Sophie had kept 'it' as a surprise for him.

"Could be I s'ppose...but we haven't seen it anywhere else...! Last night there was an old fashioned type of marquee, a really big sandy coloured canvas tent, bit like something you see on films about safaris in Africa early last century, it was just down there! I went in it! It was just past the alleyway near that merry-go-round and that steam organ thingy, *but...it's not there...Now...!* Surely they wouldn't move such a big thing after just one night! – W*ould they?!*" Disappointment filling her voice.

"I dunno Soph', could be all sorts o' reasons – look – let's go an' 'ave a ride on that big merry-go-round, looks brilliant!...And then y'can ask one o' the lads there workin' on it, they must know. 'Ere, tell you what - there's room in the 'elmet bag for the vase if y'want, y'gonna need both hands on that ride!"

"Yeah, ok, why not! Good idea! - They must know – *I hope!*".

As Jake leaned forwards to slide the bag off his shoulder, a sudden inexplicable sensing of danger erupted inside her and made her glance quickly over his back, behind him. The same furtive man she'd seen before was with another one now, they were standing side by side, just staring malevolently at them from an alleyway's shadows, only twenty feet or so away. She immediately sensed and felt a dull, threatening menace in their penetrating gaze. She realised, somehow sensing, that her awareness of tangible danger was definitely radiating from the two men. In a forced loudish whisper she said slightly panicky: *"Jake! Jake! - Quick – look behind you, quick!"*

"Eh?! What? *What's up Soph'?"* He asked her whilst mid way in disentangling his arm from the bag's strap, but hearing the change in her voice and then when he saw the frightened expression on her face, he spun around rapidly, still semi crouched, in a fighter's stance, to look behind him, the bag now forgotten, lying on the grass. His quick movement blocked Sophie's view for just a milli second, and she stepped to his side to see...that the two men weren't there any more...!

"What is it Soph? Whadidya see?" Jake asked her staring to

his front, then all around him, his voice a low growl.

"They've gone! *H,How..?! Th,there were two men just there...!*" She pointed, "they were just staring at us, their eyes were all black, horrible...scary...and I saw one of 'em just now, *right behind us*, well, just before we stopped, but he ran off, I think he, they...were...they must've been following us...*their eyes...horrible all black eyes!*" It was obvious to Jake that she was suddenly a lot more than just a bit scared.

"RIGHT! OKAY! Stay there a sec', I'll go see, but they're not there now...Just stay 'ere right in the middle o' this path, keep an eye on't bag – don't move! - *I'LL JUST BE A SEC' THAT'S ALL, OKAY?!*"

Before Sophie could reply to him he'd run quickly over to where she had pointed, less than the width of a tennis court away. Two family groups walking towards the merry-go-round moved aside rather promptly for the fast moving large man wearing a black leather bike jacket, a man with a fierce expression on his face and huge bunched fists who looked as if he was about to charge down a barn door. Jake skidded to a stop at the opening of a long, narrow and shadowy alleyway between two huge trucks, he looked down it, empty, nobody, no threat there, then he looked all around him, but no one was trying to hide or seemed suspicious to him. Hands on hips he paced around the general area, his height enabling him to see over other people's heads, but as he hadn't seen the two men he didn't know exactly who to look for. Shaking his head he looked over to Sophie and quickly moved back to her in long strides.

"They're not there now, they've gone Soph'. What did they look like?"

"They, they just looked like a couple of, well, middle aged, older men, in dark longish jackets, but...but, their eyes...horrible....evil black staring eyes..." She shuddered, more aware now of the dull headachy feeling that had started when she saw them, and looked into their eyes. Jake placed both his large hands on her trembling shoulders as he stood in front of her, looking down into her upturned and frightened face.

"Buggas must've legged it down that alley when y'spotted 'em an' I turned round. Didn't want to go down it an' leave y'ere on your own."

"Oh Jake, I don't know...I sensed something really scary...what's...do you think we should go...back..leave?" She said timorously.

"Eh! - No Way Maaan!" He jovially bellowed out loud to try to dispel her obvious fear and upset, and then with a deep breath to summon up his courage he clutched her upto his chest easily lifting her off the ground in a big hug, and summoning up even more of his reserves of bravery he planted an exaggerated kiss on the crown of her head!

His jovial bellowing continued, as he hugged her tightly. "You're with Jake The Protector! Jake One O' The Mighty Yorkshire Men! Jake...The...the bloke, the bloke who, who, really really...." his voice volumed down almost to a whisper, and Sophie, safely snuggled and wrapped in his strong arms, feeling his heart beat rapidly as she was pressed against his black leather clad chest, tipped her head back, her pale blue eyes beseechingly peeked up at him from beneath her long lashes, her shiny black hair all mussed up around her face, all her fears and that headachy feeling all gone in an instant, and in a girly coquettish whisper asked him, "Jake The Bloke who....What..?!"

"Er...Jake The...the bloke who actually, who well, er, who really likes you Soph', er... if that's ok, hope you, er, don't mind 'cause..." He didn't finish because Sophie had pushed her face up and quickly kissed him on his lips!

His eyes widened with delighted surprise. "And I'm Sophie The Yorkshire Girl, who really really likes Jake, Jake - The Mighty Yorkshire Man!". She said smiling at him, a sudden intense affection for him flooding through her.

"You D' Man!" And she kissed him again. But then, sighing deeply, she lowered her gaze and slowly, theatrically said, "Buuutt, but..Jake...*it's just that...*"

"Huuuh? *But?* B,B,But what Soph'..?" A stuttering anxiety suddenly filling his voice.

"But...It, it's just that – well - *you're crushing me!* C,C,C, can't breathe..!!" She gasped in a pretence of struggling for air.

"OH I'M SORRY!!" He exclaimed, and immediately sprung his arms open wide, causing Sophie to unceremoniously drop a couple of feet to the ground and stagger slightly, nearly dropping the glass vase. Jake quickly reached out to steady her.

"OH! OH 'ECK! I'm Sorry Soph', I..." Genuine concern for her oozing from him.

Smiling widely she carefully put the glass vase onto the grass between them and then grasped both his hands with hers, or as much as she could of them with hers being so much smaller, looked up into his eyes and her smile turned into a giggle, then a chuckle, and so too did Jake, until they were both laughing uproariously together again, causing people passing by them to smile as they saw a couple who were clearly in a very happy world all of their own.

Finally, Sophie said, "C'mon, my Big Man! I'll put the vase

safe in the bag and then let's go for a ride on that merry-go-round, and...and see where it takes us!"

As they walked towards the merry-go-round hand in hand Sophie mused to herself that last night coming here to the Fair had changed, well, everything for her - and so too had tonight! It had changed well - everything again as well! But the centre of that change for her tonight was called...Jake. And whirling around that bright centre were some wonderful feelings she hadn't ever felt before.

The huge merry-go-round had conveniently just stopped as they got to it, and people were gleefully and noisily getting off the brightly painted, almost life sized horses - that were actually unicorns with shiny golden horns, dozens of them, all fixed in position side by side, four deep around the perimeter. Sophie suggested that Jake sat on the outside one as it would seem to go faster, and she would ride on the inner one next to him. He agreed, and felt, although he didn't say it to her, that might be better anyway as she wouldn't be so exposed then as she would've been on the outer one...

The loud speakers were booming out Dion's rock n' roll hit

'The Wanderer' whilst they waited for the ride to start. They were sharing an almost childlike excitement and anticipation of fun together, as lots of other riders quickly climbed aboard all around them. Every time Sophie wasn't looking at him for a moment or two he rapidly scanned his eyes round the area, but he didn't see any sign of two men looking like she'd described.

Unknown to him however, there were now four men, all fairly similar in appearance, and they had split up to surround the merry-go-round from a distance away, to watch unseen, hidden in the surrounding crowds.

A teenaged ride attendant dressed like a 1950's teddy-boy, minus the drape coat but wearing a midnight blue waistcoat with silver thread embroided half moons on the front over a white shirt with the sleeves rolled up, and a black bootlace tie, eventually approached Jake who paid for them both, the coins going into a very worn old brown leather coin satchel around his waist.

He was starting to move away when Sophie, holding on with one hand to the gold coloured thick vertical barley twist pole that held her unicorn in place, leaned backwards and waved to him to catch his attention and shouted over the loud music, "Excuse me!", the ride attendant moved nimbly towards her in his 'brothel creeper' blue suede shoes, he bent slightly so that his head was sideways on to hers to hear her over the music.

"D'y'know what happened to the marquee - the big tent - that was over there last night?" She asked him, flicking her hand to point behind her.

He quickly stood up straight on hearing this, a strange look on his face, and replied, surprising her with his broad cockney accent, "Urr, ah dunno luv, it just went loike...", and shrugged his shoulders, he seemed as if he was about to turn away from her, but then he gave her a slightly unfocused strange looking stare and leaned in to her again and said quickly, "..Arsk our Eddie over there after y'ride – ee knows", and flicked his young Elvis styled, brylcreemed hair, in the direction of another teenaged ride attendant. This other one was standing some distance away in the middle of the broad merry-go-round by a wide, circular, pillar like console which was mostly covered in small mirrors like a disco ball, to reflect and splash over everyone all the coloured flashing lights, and it was where all the controls for the ride were.

"Oh, right! Okay, er, thanks..!"* She said, as he then moved quickly away to collect the fares from the riders behind them.

Jake looked over to her, a shadow of concern on his face, mouthing "You okay?", she nodded positively to him and then looked over to where 'Eddie' was. He could have been a twin of the attendant she'd just briefly spoken with, dressed the same as well, except his waistcoat was a lighter blue.

'Eddie' was also looking at her, and as she caught his eye he smiled and nodded imperceptibly at her, before turning away to pull a long lever down which started the ride. Her white painted wooden unicorn bucked under her, rising up smoothly and then down again, so she grabbed at the pole with both hands - and then they were off! They started to move round, and up and down at the same time, gathering speed rapidly, the music soundtrack went up in volume and changed to The Doors': 'Riders On The Storm'.

It was fun and it was surreal. Everything beyond the ride and all around them quickly became just flashing blurs of bright colours as they spun round and round and up and down, her unicorn was moving very quickly and she was forced to lean out towards Jake as the centripetal force built up. It's like going round a never ending corner at speed on the bike she thought.

Her long black hair flew out behind her, and she felt as if she and Jake, and all the other riders with them, really were on magical beasts for real, galloping away all together on a long journey through a dark forest lit up by flashes of rainbow coloured lights in the middle of the night...as if they were part of the Faerie host.

The ride eventually slowed and finally stopped. The loud music was now the original Noel Harrison song: 'The Windmills Of Your Mind', *"Oh I love this song!"* Sophie shouted excitedly over to Jake, *"I loved that ride too! Did you?!"*

*"Aye, I did, it were ace!...*Years since I've been on one!" Jake said, a big grin on his face. Even though they were in the midst

of a melee of people now dismounting and moving away from their rides, and others who were moving in to take their places all around them, Sophie saw the teddy-boy teenager called Eddie, still over in the middle area, point to her and Jake and then rapidly beckon them over to go to him.

At the same time Jake was helping her to get off the unicorn safely, as they were both a bit dizzy.

"Jake, I think it's him..."

Jake immediately tensed, his grey eyes suddenly hard as flint.

"Where?" He growled.

"No, *not him, not them*, from before – *him!* - That lad over there, he's called Eddie, that other one I asked before the ride, it's his brother, he told me he'd know about the marquee....I think it could be, could it be - that he's the one who the gypsy lady meant, you remember - *who wanted to see us...?!"*

"Urrrh?" He said uncertainly, looking over towards Eddie

48

who was now beckoning to them even more rapidly, as the crowd was starting to thin out. Sophie said, "I think it is, I think, I think we should see...can we..?"

"Okaaay..." Jake said slowly, not quite sure, letting out a deep breath. "But only if y'really want to...Only if y're sure Soph', *'cause I think there's summat funny goin' on 'ere tonight!*"

Taking her hand in his he lead the way, in a don't-mess-with-me strut over to confront the lad called Eddie.

"Noice one folks! C'mon then, in 'ere quick, sharpish like, *in 'ere...'fore they see us...!*" He had the same strong cockney accent as his brother, and quickly opened a narrow, mirror covered, cleverly disguised doorway in the centre console structure as he was speaking.

"Y'What?! Who are you then mate?! What d'y'want..wh...?"

Jake aggressively confronted the lad called Eddie, who looked to him like an extra from the old rock n' roll film 'That'll

Be The Day'.

Interrupting Jake he spoke rapidly, *"It's s'alright mate, it's s'alright!* I'm Eddie mate, you're Jake an' she's Sophie! Magda told me y'wuz 'ere! *Now c'mon quick 'fore they see us...!"*

And then he disappeared through the small open doorway. Jake and Sophie looked at each other bemusedly, Sophie shrugged her shoulders and said, *"In for a penny...?"*

Jake sighed, "Aye alright then! - But I'll go first, y'never know.."

Eddie was already several steps down a steepish, narrow wooden stairway beyond the small doorway as Jake squeezed himself sideways and ducked under it, still holding Sophie's hand, his other hand clenched into a hard fist in readiness in front of him.

"G'steady folks, 's a bit narro' 'ere, gets wider soon tho'", Eddie said to them over his shoulder.

The door behind them closed on its own as soon as they had

both passed through it with a surprisingly heavy clunk for what had just seemed like a flimsy wooden panel door. The descending stepped tunnel was dimly lit by red lights concealed in the wooden steps' risers. The walls and ceiling were earth. Sophie thought it was just like a big rabbit hole – as per the one at the beginning of one of her favourite stories from childhood - 'Alice In Wonderland…!'

An absorbing silence had suddenly enveloped them, as all the noise from the outside world had been immediately shut out when the door had closed. The only sounds for the next half a minute or so came from the three of them going down the steps, until they heard Eddie's reassuring voice, from some distance away below them, which was slightly muffled now by the earthen tunnel.

"*...Good Oh! - We're nearly there na folks, it's just dahn 'ere....*" He was about a dozen or so steps below them, "*...Rightio then... an' 'ere we are...!* Just 'ang on a sec'...na then...*where's mi key..?*"

He'd stopped at another door at the bottom of the passage,

which had widened out as he'd said it would, but this door was an oversized very solid looking old wooden one with black metal riveted studs all over it, supported by three very strong looking but ornately scrolled wrought iron hinges, a large, shiny brass keyhole was right in the middle of it.

Fumbling in his trouser pocket, he pulled out a long heavy shiny brass key – that seemed far too large to have ever fitted in his black, tight fitting, 'drain-pipe' style trousers...he inserted it carefully in to the keyhole, and using both hands twisted it clockwise once, then twice. The sounds of heavy metallic rattling came from within the door as several locks opened up simultaneously, and then, pushing it with his shoulder, the large, heavy and imposing door opened halfway with a loud creaking...

Sophie and Jake had caught up with him by now, Sophie huddled up behind Jake, thinking that the door looked and sounded like something from a Hammer Horror film, she gripped Jake's hand even tighter.

"That's funny! – It don't normally make that noise when...

Ah!...*I know why...!* - *Anyway* - right then, good 'oh, we meddit, all safe n' sound like, an' 'ere we all are as promised!" Eddie said with relief, and walked through into the bright white light now spilling out from the half open doorway.

CHAPTER 3:

The 'Trocadero Coffee Bar'

As soon as Eddie had opened the door Jake and Sophie heard a scratchy record playing 'Strangers On The Shore', by Acker Bilk, over a babble of voices from a group of people talking.

"'Ello, 'ello again everybody...!" Eddie cheerfully greeted whomever was in the room beyond....

Jake looked at Sophie with an even more bewildered expression on his face. Now that Eddie had gone in he started to cautiously poke his head around the door to see who and what was in there...then peering around the edge of the door and actually seeing what lay beyond it he gasped, and froze...motionless.

Sophie squeezed upto his side, hanging onto his arm, and

peered in as well.

"OH! Oh My God..!" She gasped.

"Bloooody 'elllll!" Jake said quietly, in obvious shock.

"...Can't be...!...Just...No Way! What the?...Can't be...!"
They both said in shocked disbelief at the scene in front of
them.

They were looking into a largish, well lit room. It was a
room that...just couldn't be there.

Because what they were looking at was the interior of a busy
1960's High Street type coffee bar with about a dozen
customers in it. They were sat on plain wooden chairs around
red formica topped tables arranged mainly along the walls but
with some in the central floor area, which was covered in blue
and white chequerboard laid lino tiles, which could've done
with a good sweep up and a good mopping.

The walls were mostly covered with unframed black and

white photographs, lots of them with autographs, of 50's and 60's singers, bands, film stars, artistes and notables of the time.

Here and there various posters, some quite faded, promoted long bygone attractions and events. Amongst them Sophie was amused to see a poster for the 1966 film 'Alfie', starring Michael Caine, the theme tune of which had run through her head this lunchtime when she'd been sitting thinking about things at the harbour.

At the far end of the cafe was a large, wide window and a glazed door which presumably, lead out onto the street beyond – wherever – whenever? - that was...They couldn't see through either though because several pale yellow venetian blinds had been pulled down over them.

A long and well worn chrome topped high countered bar with a white tiled frontage below glass shelves displaying chunky cut slices of a variety of cakes and unwrapped biscuits on pale yellow plates ran for almost the full length of the room on the left hand side. A big complicated antique looking chrome and brass coffee machine leaked hissing steam from various parts of itself, emitting a fragrant aroma of coffee, and it dominated the middle area of the counter. An oversized, colourfully lit and ornate Whurlitzer jukebox squatted by the wall opposite to it from which the record they could hear was playing.

"Aaah! 'Ello! Nah then! 'Ows it goin' Eddie?! - An' a Big Welcome to You Two!" A man's slightly milder cockney accent than Eddie's called out to them from behind the counter. He was a tall, thin man, with black greased back hair, wearing a once white but now coffee stained serving apron who loudly greeted them. He'd had his back partly to them as he reached for a tray and cups and saucers, from the haphazardly stacked piles of matching pale yellow crockery on the back wall of shelves behind the bar. He'd been partly obscured from their view at first by the tall counter and the steam emitting Heath Robinson-esq coffee machine, and he'd just turned round quickly, holding a tray with two coffee cups and saucers on it in his hands.

"Two coffees?...Any cakes?...Biccies?...No?...Just two coffees then.?" He asked Jake and Sophie. Before they could even think about replying, stunned as they were, Eddie quickly butted in and said, "Yeh, yeh, goin' good, cheers Alfie, but now ah'd best get meself back up sharpish - *cum' in you two, grab a seat, an' 'ave a coffee..."*

Having quickly said all that in one breath he edged past Jake and Sophie, both still slack jawed in shock by the door, they heard him dashing back up the wooden stairs behind them as they continued staring wide eyed into the room.

"Yes, dooo come in! Come in! Plenty o' room! Join the party! I'll 'ave y'coffees ready in a sec...grab a seat, wherever y'want..." The man behind the counter, Alfie, called out to them with effusive bonhomie – and Sophie thought how strange was it that that name had cropped up again?!

Compared to the surreal impossibility of all of this, it was the contrast of the sheer normalcy of these first few moments which further brain scrambled Jake and Sophie. But she was the first to partly recover. Still clutching Jake's arm she stepped hesitantly into the room glancing curiously at all the people sat around who had been chatting and drinking their coffees. Their conversations had abruptly stopped when they came in, and now they were just sitting relaxed, most of them smiling as they looking back at her and Jake.

She looked up into Jake's dumbstruck face and then back to the man behind the counter, before saying but not quite recognizing her own voice when she did, because which, understandably, sounded a bit croaky, *"Er, yes please...er, wh, what, where...?"*

"Good Oh! An' Fret Not! All will be revealed soon! - *Ol' Mr S.'ll be 'ere inna bit an' ee'll be explainin' fings* - I'll just do you y'coffees first tho'...*Ouch! Sod it! Bloomin' thing!"* He exclaimed as a little jet of steam zapped his thumb as he put their cups onto the machine, he shook his hand in the air to cool it before he stuck his thumb in his mouth, then wiped it on the front of his apron.

Despite herself Sophie pinched her lips together to mask an amused smile at his comedic antics and demeanour, and lead Jake towards two chairs close by at an empty table. The large door behind them creaked as it closed. Jake glanced over his shoulder but it had blended in with the rest of the décor. You'd never know now that it'd been there, he thought. Conversation quickly resumed amongst the other people in the room, after they had all nodded or half waved in friendly greetings to the two new arrivals.

"Well - You did say you: 'thought there was something funny going on tonight' Jake!" She said to him in a low voice, and quickly put her hand over her mouth as she stifled a laugh..."But this, *this is more than funny - it's mad!!"*

Jake slowly turned his head to look at her, and just as quietly said, "Pinch me 'ard an' tell me I'm really 'ere, that this is really..."

"Aaaand 'Ere We Are...! Two coffees cumin' right up!... Milk n' sugar's on't tray for yers!" Alfie called out dramatically, waltzing over to them between the other tables, holding a circular wooden tray up high with skilful ease on the fingertips of one hand, and with a flourish he spiralled it down and slid it carefully onto the table in front of them.

"Nah then, ah've got to say...'case y'wunderin' loike – *that* y're not in Fairyland...! An' ah'm not a big fairy...! *Known a few tho' in mi time I 'ave...I can tell yus!"* He said grinning at the cheeky double entendre.

"Anyways...Y'll know the story – *never accept anyfink to eat or drink in Fairyland!* - 'Cause if y'do then y'll never be able to leave..right? Well, y're both ok in 'ere, 'cos y're in 'The Trocadero Coffee Bar'! Opened it meself...long time ago now that was...So - Enjoy!...Finest coffee in...*where are we t'night?!* - Oh yes, Scarrrrborough! Lovely town! - 'Ere!- D'y'know I remember us all goin' to see Adam Faith at The Spa 'ere when he first got started, on 'oliday we were, stayed at Butlins for a week, me an' young Eddie n' Bert 'is brother...eeeh! *We 'ad some laughs that week we did...is it still just as busy..?"*

Jake and Sophie could only stare at him, slack jawed again, at this chatty outpouring, utterly flabbergasted, before Jake managed to say, "Erm, well, er, no, no mate, it's not now...sorry, but it, it shut...while back...*Butlins...*"

"Oh! *Well!...Did it?!* Oh! - *Well that's a right shame now innit, lot o'fun we 'ad there we did!"* And with that he

61

wandered back behind the counter, muttering to himself about *'it being a right shame...'*

"But that, that was *decades* ago Jake!" Sophie whispered, "He's talking about the late fifties early sixties...must've been! But he's, he's not old enough! I'd say he's only in his thirties... and that Eddie and his brother Bert...they're, well, they're only...teenagers...!"

Jake cautiously picked up his coffee cup, staring into it warily and sniffing it, and just before it reached his lips he quietly said to her out of the side of his mouth, "If the next record on that jukebox is the theme-tune from 'Tales O' The Unexpected' – *we're definitely outta here...!*"

It wasn't. With an electronic hum, click and whirr, and then a few seconds of scratchy sounds, it was: 'My Generation' by 'The Who'. They sipped at their coffees, looking around them, slowly taking it all in. After a few minutes, as the jukebox quietened, the sounds of a chair scraping back on the floor, caused by a lady getting to her feet whilst tapping a coffee cup with a spoon caught their and everyone else's attention, and all the conversations stopped, the room becoming quiet, apart from the occasional hiss from the coffee machine.

A lady was now standing up by a table in the corner where she'd been sitting on her own. She had the same reddish auburn coloured hair as gypsy Magda Leah Rose but it was cut much shorter and pulled back into a neat bun, and she also had the same sparkling emerald green eyes. There the similarities ended, this lady was younger looking and dressed in a very modern dark bottle green well tailored business suit of jacket and skirt, over a creamy blouse, with a large shiny clear crystal brooch at her throat. Sophie, taking all this in in a glance, guessed that she would probably be in her mid forties.

Putting the spoon back down onto a saucer the lady opened her hands out widely to greet all those present in the room, and then with a lovely smile of exceptional warmth that seemed to glow as it radiated from her face, she said:

"W e l c o m e...Everyone..."

Her voice was gentle, educated, even a bit posh, but just

those two spoken words from her conveyed such a warm friendliness to everyone in the room, such an immediate putting-at-ease, that on hearing it even Jake seemed to relax a fraction, but he still held Sophie's hand tightly.

The standing lady then clasped her hands together in front of her and continued,

"...And a very good evening to you all, my name is Maria, and I'm a friend and colleague of Anders, I just want to explain *what* it is you're experiencing right now, and *why*...before Anders gets here – he's just told me he's been delayed but he should be arriving any minute now".

She looked around the room at everyone. "I can see that some of you who weren't at the marquee last night to listen to him give his talk have come with friends tonight who were, and so you are...perhaps..." She paused and smiled enigmatically, "...here because you were...meant to be...now.

"Anders is coming again tonight to explain things in some greater detail for all of you...and I'm sure you will all have lots of questions for him later!"

Jake tilted his head closer to Sophie, his lips brushing the hair covering her ears and whispered, *"So is it this 'Anders' who you saw...heard...went to...last night then Soph'?"*

"Yes...it was, and he was amazing!' She whispered back. "What he said, it was like a, like a catalyst for me, changed everything so quickly...That's why I wanted to listen and, and learn some more again tonight...even meet and talk with him - but with you as well...so you could as well...I, *I wanted it to be a surprise for you,* 'cos I thought, I hoped, *that you'd be amazed as well!"* She turned her head further round to look into his grey eyes, her pale blue ones brimming with happy and hopeful tears.

Jake just smiled and nodded in understanding, thinking that *it was certainly a surprise!* – But if Sophie felt like that it was more than good enough for him! He leaned into her to nuzzle her ear with his nose to assuage any doubts he thought she might have about his reaction, and then leaning back, he let go of her hand and put his arm around her shoulders and held her tightly to him, stretching his long legs out under their table.

Maria said, "the reason we aren't in the marquee tonight but in 'The Trocadero' instead – *and thank you so much again for this Alfie...*" She smiled over to Alfie who bashfully replied, *"Oh!...S'alright! Always glad to 'elp! Y'all know that! Anytime Maria! 'Tis the work of a moment to put a 'Private Party' sign up in't window an' pull the blinds down!"*

"Thank you, you're always so very kind and so very helpful to us all..."

Returning her gaze to encompass the room again, she continued, "...the reason is because we had to quickly move the marquee to...well, somewhere else, because those who are opposed to what we are doing and what is happening now *on* this planet found it rather sooner than we expected..."

She sighed lightly, looked down at her hands for a moment, then looked back up, her brilliant smile back again on her lips.

"We always hope that some of the visitors who were drawn to

us in the first place come back of course, and it's wonderful that more and more people all over your World who are now waking up do just that...and so, with the marquee gone we set up this portal in an alternative time line, for those of you who did manage to come again tonight."

A youth sitting near to Sophie and Jake asked Maria, "...I'd've thought a lot more people would've come back tonight though than just us, even assuming not everyone who did thought to ask about the marquee at the merry-go-round...?"

"Yes, you are right, quite right, I'm quite sure, in fact I know they did." Maria replied.

"But tonight we couldn't risk having this portal's access point open for very long, the, the...opposition, have obviously improved their technology very recently to detect them much more rapidly now, but in another twenty four hours or so we should be able to block them from doing that, we are working on it as I speak! But...fortunately...you all came through in the period that we could keep it open! And of course when you leave here later another one will take you back to the Fair, but not back to the merry-go-round, in fact, regardless of how long it will seem that you have been here in Alfie's cafe tonight, and then later, perhaps, for those of you who want to...go somewhere else – you'll all get back to the Fair just a few seconds after you left it to come here...!"

Gasps, exclamations of astonishment, surprise, and concern had erupted a few moments ago at what Maria had said, the volume of all those outbursts were now much louder from everyone on hearing all this as well.

Sophie took her mobile out of her jacket pocket, glanced at it and then showed it to Jake saying, "Look – there's no signal...!"

Jake took his out, looked at it, and showed her his 'no signal' icon as well, and he said quietly to her, "Bloody 'ell Soph'! I *was* right! – Talk about 'Tales O' The Unexpected'...it's now 'The Twilight Zone'...!

And then, so he could be heard above the noise and clamour of everyone else talking, he loudly, but politely addressed

Maria.

"Er, *'scuse me!*...Maria!...But who or what is this 'opposition'? - 'Cause Soph' 'ere reckons we were followed tonight, at the Fair, I chased 'em off, well, I think I did – but they'd vanished – I didn't actually see 'em, but she saw two of 'em, two blokes, *'they 'ad 'orrible black eyes'* she said, an' earlier, right when we'd more or less just got to the Fair a gypsy lady came out of 'er caravan, *and she knew our names!* An' she warned us about some that *'aren't from 'ere'* – so what, just what was she and now you...*on about?* 'Cause I can look after meself – *but no way I'm 'avin' Soph' put in any danger...an' if...!*"

A man's cultured voice behind Jake answered him... *"A Very, Very Good Question Indeed! - And, if I may say so, one followed by a most Admirable Proclamation!"*

Sophie instantly recognized the man's voice that came from behind her to interrupt Jake. Heads turned and all eyes fixed onto the man who must have come through the same door that Jake and Sophie had come through, but which had opened unnoticed by them, any creaking it had made must have been masked by the noise of all the voices in the room Jake thought.

"And one that I will most certainly endeavour to answer for you quite soon young man!"

He was now walking over to the coffee bar counter, as all the voices in the room petered out. He was wearing the same, which Sophie thought, was a very old fashioned styled three piece greeny-brown faint tartan tweed suit and tie, with brown leather brogue shoes polished to a high shine. In fact, despite the mop of blond hair, with his general looks, voice and age, he still reminded her a lot of the actor Alistair Simm in one of those classic old British black and white Ealing Studio films that she so loved watching, curled up on the sofa with a takeaway, one where he was an old school headmaster, or some other more-than-slightly eccentric, elderly and prominent personage!

Jake swivelled his head round from looking at the man to look at Sophie with his eyebrows raised and quietly asked her, *"Is he - who you mean…?"*

She nodded rapidly saying just as quietly, *"Yes! That's him!"*

A big part of Jake was then actually quite relieved. He hadn't quite liked to admit it to himself before but he had been a mite concerned, even a teeny bit jealous perhaps of this man that Sophie had seemed so enthralled by. But now he had actually seen this apparently harmless looking doddery old chap who looked of an age that would make him her grandfather, all those uneasy thoughts quickly evaporated, and he relaxed a little more, and smiled wryly to himself.

Nodding in a friendly greeting to Alfie, the man extended his arm over the counter and shook his hand vigorously, saying a few quietly spoken words to him. He then turned, and waved in greeting over to Maria saying, "Maria! *Lovely to see you! Thank you so much* for holding the fort in your more than capable hands!" Maria smiled affectionately back at him in reply and sat back down.

He then addressed everyone in the room saying, "...It would seem that I've arrived just in time to answer a very important question! *So...where to begin?*" He said lowering his head in thought as he leaned back with his elbows behind him resting on the bar top. His head suddenly snapped up and a wide friendly grin spread across his face, and with it an aura of bonhomie and a gentle but immense power of goodness radiated from him, deeply touching all those present. His smile was infectious, and Jake noticed that he as well as everyone else was also smiling along with him.

"Well, *Firstly though*...I'd better introduce myself to you all hadn't I?! And to some of you again! Hello everybody! You are all most, most welcome! My name is Anders Starrmann and I'm delighted to be here with you all today! And please accept my sincere apologies for keeping you all waiting - one thing and another crops up from time to time! Ha! - Pun intended! And - I'm especially delighted to be meeting you all here *in this excellent establishment* - 'The Trocadero Cafe'! *My goodness!* I remember the opening night! *What a night that was eh Alfie?!*" He said looking over his shoulder to Alfie.

"*It certainly was Mr. S!* A right good ol' knees up we all 'ad that night we did!" He replied respectfully.

"Yes, we certainly did! - And 'The Trocadero' has gone from strength to strength ever since! *Well done to you ol'chap!*"

Alfie beamed at the praise. "Well everyone, I think, to start off, before I can get to the actual specifics of answering that first question, I'm going to have to explain, in much more detail than I did yesterday evening, the context - the relevant background to all that is happening first, and which, I must say, I intended to do this evening anyway, before I can really answer your question." He said nodding over to Jake, acknowledging him.

"I know that some of you heard some of this background, and indeed, some more general relevant things that are all part of this last night, but some of you didn't, so if I could beg your patience I'd like to set the scene again – but in a little more detail and closer up focus now, for you all...In fact, *just like my old friend Max used to say...*", and he pointed to a signed black and white photograph of Max Bygraves that was fixed with yellowing sellotape, amongst the many other photos onto the wall near the door he had come in from, *"...I'm gonna tell you a story...!"*

And so, taking a deep breath, Anders Starrmann began...

"Do you remember the last time that you had a, *a feeling*, or, a vague *intuition* about something? - About something you wanted to know, something you wanted to happen, or something about an important decision that you were going to have to make of what's best for you to do? Or...it could have been something you just felt you ought to do as soon as possible, or somewhere you just felt you ought to go to...?

"...Then, and perhaps, due to all of the ever present and many distractions of your everyday life, those feelings and thoughts got put to the back of your mind, or at least to the back of your everyday conscious mind. But then...a while later, it could've been an hour, a day, or a week - you then - let's say, just for the moment, let's use the word: by *'coincidence'*, you met someone, you read something, you came across something, or you went somewhere *'by chance'*. And that lead you closer to the answer that you were seeking, or even...to you actually finding out, realising, or even manifesting that, that answer, that result you wanted...!

"...And then, eventually, when you had that great feeling of suddenly knowing the answer or actually experiencing that

74

thing you were wanting and seeking, that achievement...that fulfilment, which may have also shown or revealed to you a more meaningful purpose, a new direction, or opportunity or *whatever...*the point is - it made you feel happy, positive, excited, more alive, and maybe, just maybe...and hopefully it did! - *It started to change, even in just a small way, your perceptions, of, well, everything..."*

He paused and nodded gratefully to Alfie for the glass of water that he had just placed discreetly by his elbow.

"So...in a nutshell - something obviously very positive and mysterious had happened! – *For you!*

"You *desired* it, and whether you were aware of it or not you then *allowed* it to happen – and so it did! It got created, and eventually it manifested!   So...in future, as and when that happens - *embrace it! Recognize it!* Realise that that whole process *is deliberate and real!*   That's Most Important! Because then, with more practice, as you keep doing that you will be well on the road to recognizing more and more of these so called *'coincidences'* when they appear - for what they really are – *because they are Your Own, Deliberate - Creations...!*

"...Now...technically speaking, there is no such thing as a 'coincidence' – *I know, I know, that might seem a bit of a contentious statement - but bear with me...*What actually happened is that it was You Yourself all along who was creating those *'events'* that you called *'coincidences'* - that eventually lead you to where you wanted to be! - *But you just didn't recognize them as part of a real, live, genuine, and natural process that you can do...!* You didn't realise that it was actually *You* having the natural ability to deliberately connect to higher frequencies in higher dimensions where you were actually creating them, and then, as time passed, you were drawing them to you here to manifest into this third dimension's frequency!

"...And so, of course, not being aware of all this, and so, therefore, not consciously looking out for them - you just didn't get to see the full picture that all those 'coincidences' or, let's call them *'event dots'* were making for you – if you had joined all those dots up...!

"...You were just seeing the individual 'event dots', just seeing them as seemingly random, inexplicable and isolated events, and perhaps, more often than not, you saw them - *and then, due to so many of life's distractions and preoccupations as well as the, let's call it - 'the social programming' you have all been subjected to throughout your lives - you just dismissed them!* So the connections you could have made, by standing back to reveal 'the bigger picture' they made by joining them all up, just like in a dot-to-dot puzzle book, they just passed by unnoticed at that time by the perceptions of your conscious mind..."

Sophie hadn't realised she'd spoken quite so loudly when she'd then said: 'so it's like looking at pixels on a screen – it's only when you move back from them that you can see the actual picture they make...?', but Anders had heard her and he said, "Absolutely right my dear! In this day and age that's probably a far more up to date comparison than my old dot-to-dot book!" He smiled at her, before taking another sip of water.

"...And now we are getting to the crux of it...The Ability that all of you here, and that all humans on this planet innately have...interestingly the word 'innately' stems from the old Latin word 'natus' – to be born – so you are born with - 'The Ability To Deliberately Create', and then to consciously recognise, perceive, be aware of - to see 'the picture' they make for you, and then to consciously and physically experience what those manifestations in 'the picture' reveal...

"...All that is quite an achievement!   But The Ability is natural to you – as I say, you were born with it…!

"...And you called all the 'event dots' leading upto that achievement you desired as just *random coincidences'* before!

"Now...it is that first stage of recognizing – of seeing with a clearer focused, higher conscious awareness and perception – which is something that all of you here tonight, and many, many others like you *on* this planet...are now...*starting to become fully conscious of* – but now with a *higher consciousness of –* once again...

"*How?   Or Why?*   You might ask!...Well, to put it simply -

because you always could do...! And, believe me, you could and can – *do so much much more besides!* And - *'Why?'* – Well...you are living now in the early stages of a period in a great cycle of time, a Great Year, called a 'Yuga'. Which, in its essence, means you are now living in the early stages of a great ebb and flow of positive cosmic energies where the planet of Earth and all the sentient life on it, is more than just starting to experience the initial flooding approach of these higher frequencies coming to them.

"Their full effect will be...and I'll use an analogy...is going to be like kick starting a cold, sluggish engine...it will take some constant ongoing efforts to...to get it running properly again, but when it does it will be like the difference between sitting on a motorcycle and pushing it along with only the power of your legs to get to your destination – *or not!* – To suddenly having its engine fire up so you can open the throttle and ride there faster and faster! It will be like a re-naissance - a re-birth, for you, and because of that the road your race is now on will take you to re-discover wonders and other fantastic abilities within you that I suggest - *you can scarcely conceive of right now!"*

Jake looked at Sophie and quietly said to her, *"now that I do understand!* I've 'ad to kick start and sometimes trundle along pushing a bike that won't fire up with me legs a few times over the years!"*

Anders had paused again to take a sip of his water, he then continued, starting though with a grimace and a morose sigh...

"But...a very long, long time ago all those myriad and wonderful abilities – that I just said 'you can scarcely conceive of right now' - that as a race you all had, *and still have,* and amongst them of course, as I've been saying, the ability to deliberately create and then to *consciously recognize and experience them* - all of those abilities that were and are ultimately intended to further your spiritual growth, your conscious evolution, and which, as a race you used quite naturally, in full conscious awareness, by default, all the time – that awareness of being able to consciously recognize and realise them was deliberately, by various means - *by a predator race that came to your planet – because they had discovered that your race had them* - and they *definitely* didn't want you to *continue realising* that you had them – let alone *consciously* use them for anyone's benefit other than their own...that *conscious awareness* of your abilities you all had...was...very effectively... *'turned off'*...by them.

"...Not *totally turned off* though, they couldn't do that, and it wasn't in their interest to do so totally even if they could. But they effectively turned it off by sufficiently altering and reducing your perceptions of 'reality' and what is truly possible just enough to suit their malign purposes...And then they managed and manipulated – you could say they *'re-wired'* - your remaining conscious perceptions, causing you to create – albeit unknowingly – so many worrisome lifestyle preoccupations and divisions amongst you. So when they achieved all of that, it made you forget, as the generations passed, that you ever had those abilities...

"...Because the beings who did this, *and are still doing this to you*, wanted and needed, to exploit, to manipulate and then ultimately – seed, farm and harvest all your abilities for their benefit alone – they desperately needed, *and still need*, the produce of that harvest that they can manipulate and engineer for themselves from those creative abilities that you all have.

"Just about your entire race *was*, and *is* used, for their own, very dark agenda...because you humans, *You Have The Ability To Deliberately Create, and they do not! They cannot! They can only only subvert and parasite off something that already exists! Like a malignant virus that needs a host body to survive in.*

"And so they corralled, divided, harnessed and used you humans as their livestock, their host body to create that vital something they need – without the vast majority of you even being aware that they were doing so...And I'll get to what that vital something for them actually is, shortly...

"These hidden creatures are malevolent predators and parasites, like energy vampires, feeding off...*you*...what *you* can create for them that is essential for their survival, they desperately need it and consume it voraciously, manipulating the human race, to unwittingly, create it for them...

"Throughout the past, and it still goes on today of course, those of you whom they couldn't and still can't corral, divide, harness, handicap, control or manipulate – the seers, the

82

mystics, the shamans, the so called 'heretics', the free thinkers, the artists and the poets - and sometimes even whole indigenous native populations whom openly used those traits, were hunted down, and, and over the centuries they were - and I'm sorry for being so blunt - but they were, and they still are often being...killed. Their demises usually being explained away these days as 'suicide' or 'unexpected but natural causes'. As well as, and this happens more and more these days, their characters and reputations being systematically ridiculed and destroyed...by using a vast array of wicked methods, from the brutal, to the insidiously subtle...

"...But Not All! *Thank Goodness!* All those who were, and are, aware of and so managed to evade the predatory vampiric parasites and their human minions, and survive their constant onslaughts...they learned how to camouflage themselves and hide, as they bravely continued working as a Resistance Movement over the centuries, against them. Truly Heroic men, women and even children, all of them..."

Anders wiped his hands over his face, his eyes moist from deep emotion.

83

Sophie looked at Jake, and he slowly turned his head to look back at her, his face paler than usual, his eyes wide, this time it was Sophie who silently mouthed *'You Okay?'* Jake just nodded, puffing his cheeks out, and was about to say something but stopped himself as Anders had taken a deep breath and had started speaking again...

"So...when they, let's say, when they gradually, over time, they 'blocked' your higher perceptions so you would be unable to realise what was happening to you – so you couldn't 'join-the-dots'..." He nodded towards Sophie saying, " - *or the pixels* - to see the 'big picture'. So then they successfully managed to harness and shackle you, to unwittingly create for them, and it resulted of course in you being unable to deliberately and consciously use all of those natural abilities you all have *for your own positive benefit at will, whenever you desired to do so – because they'd 'blocked' you from realising that you had them!*

"Even if, by then, as I've just said, the majority, the masses of you even knew or even slightly remembered that you had The Ability. And to maintain you in that required state of ignorance the predators constantly used, and still use, ongoing insidious propaganda, through Governments and a horde of other Manipulative Institutions. They use them for social programming and many, many other sophisticated techniques – and in this present age increasingly so by technology - to control your minds and your perceptions, and therefore your beliefs, to hide from you your true creative reality...and ultimately the awareness of - what you all *really are*...

"Interestingly, the one word of 'Government' stems from the two ancient Greek words: 'To Rule', and 'The Mind'...

"...Let me give you another analogy – try considering it like this...You could compare what happened, this 'Fall Of Man' as it has been called by some, to, as time passed, putting one veil after another over a very brightly shining lamp in an immense and lovely room in a magnificent, stately mansion of infinite size, that you were happy to move around in, to live in, and you really enjoyed being there. But, with every veil put over the lamp in the the room you were in, it, of course, got gradually darker, and darker in there, the shadows deeper. So the room seemed to get smaller and smaller, and you saw less and less of all the wonders in that beautiful, immense room...and almost completely forgot that it was *just one of the rooms* in a huge, infinite mansion...Your manipulated perception effectively trapped you in there...The exit Doors of Perception to other rooms were by now, hidden in the shadows, and forgotten about...

"...Until...eventually, as so much time had passed by, you got so used to what appeared to be just a small empty room that was so dim, shadowy and grim, and thus seemed more than a little frightening. Each generation born into it was told by the previous generation that it was just the normal state of the room you had to live in, and everything around you...was the normal state of things...and they told you: '...so get used to it, get on with it and just accept it, that's just the way it is...!'

"Which of course, is exactly what those placing the veils had wanted, planned, and then managed to deceive you into thinking, perceiving and so believing...all along...

"...Part of that veiled lamp analogy was from the writings of an author I first met in the early nineteen sixties called Arthur

Chesterton, a chap who was publishing much detailed research into the hidden hands behind world events. I think it was in one of his later books - 'The New Unhappy Lords', if I remember correctly...or was it in...? Mmmm...*anyway* - please do research his writings when you get the opportunity to...his work was very insightful, factual and educative.

"Not the least for his writings being so because it was uncontaminated by the modern 'Political Correctness Speak'. Another author, George Orwell, whose real name was Eric Blair, predicted the 'Political Correctness' speak in his book published in nineteen forty-nine called: 'Nineteen Eighty Four'. The book gives a sinister prediction of the future, which has, today, almost become a reality. In the book he says that 'Newspeak' will become the only acceptable language. It is the same thing, 'Political Correctness Speak' and 'Newspeak' are linguistic designs meant to limit freedom of thought, limit self-identity, limit self-expression, limit freewill, and limit anything that ideologically threatens The Governing State, and all its Manipulative Institutions...So - there's more reading for you all if you haven't already read it!

"The veiled lamp analogy does tie in rather well to a tale by the philosopher Plato, who was born in classical Greece around four hundred and twenty four B.C. Plato was the founder of 'The Academy' in Athens, the first institution of higher learning in the western world. His work I want to refer you to is called: 'Plato's Cave'.

"Plato's Cave, in a brief summary I'll do for you now, tells an allegorical story of people kneeling and chained together in a dark cave with a fire behind them that casts dancing shadows onto the wall in front of them. Those shadows are all they can see...

"And so, as much time passes, their previous memories of being able to see other things, before they were brought to the cave, fade away. Now they think that the flickering shadows on the wall - which are just about all they have been able to see for such a long, long time...they think, then they come to believe, that the moving shadows and the narrow cave they are all chained in are now their only reality...Then, amazingly one day a man escapes! He ignores all the clamorous shouting from the others for him to come back, and not to go away, and just keep looking at the shadows...! But he ignores them and crawls out to the entrance of the cave where he sees the bright sun in a blue summer sky, green fields stretching away to the faraway horizons and many other wonderful things *on* the Earth...But the man is so shocked and frightened by the unfamiliarity, the strangeness, and the vastness of what he sees in front of him, so he quickly crawls back into the cave, gets back into his chains, and then carries on just staring at the shadows on the wall...along with everyone else...

"There are several versions of Plato's Cave with different endings, but we'll stick with that one for today, as essentially that is the central message contained in all of them.

"...Indeed, never have truer words also been written than those by the great French poet Charles Baudelaire, who died in eighteen sixty seven, he wrote:

'...never forget...that the devil's greatest trick has been to persuade you - that he doesn't exist...!'

"...Another analogy, going back again to the veiled lamp...is that you could say it was like installing powerful negative filters over your true *positive* awareness, insight, intuition and perception. Filters that also, very effectively, blocked out your *positive* motivations to deliberately, consciously create and experience *positive manifestations* as well, which used to help you in *en-abling* your access to the infinitely higher realms of your perceptive consciousness - that previously, before those *dis-abling* filters were installed, you could do by default, and enjoyed and thought that doing so was quite natural, and you knew how to access them whenever you wanted to...

"...So...the ongoing results of all of this: the 'almost fully turning off', the drastic reduction of the sense of what you perceive is possible, the filtering, the dimming, the blocking, the dumbing down, the enforced limitation, the shackling, the farming, the harvesting, and down to all the negative manifestations of everyday petty and irrelevant preoccupying distractions all designed to further *mislead* you - *at the very least* - and to cull you *at their very worst* - those ongoing results can be seen manifested in events to constantly create and maintain the discordant, dystopic world around you, that seethes with so much negativity to this day...

"...That is the theme and the manifestation of the picture, the 'reality', the parasites want. So they have used and manipulated you as a host species to unknowingly, by the general masses of humanity, to create it for them...

"...*Because the results of all the seemingly random events in this manifested picture, this manifested false and phantom reality, create an energy for them, a powerful Negative Energy. It is the very low frequency of negative energy that they devour, they gorge on, they feed off, it is their sustenance, it is essential nourishment for them - because they are parasitic negative energy vampires...*

"...And their picture, their desired reality, will only be completely manifested when your entire planet's vibrational frequency in this level of the third dimension has been so lowered that *they will be able to fully, and physically manifest into it*, from the regions where they exist now in only a non-physical form...

"...Part of the process of making the planet's surface more conducive to the lower frequencies they require is called 'terraforming', which in reality is 'terra' - which means earth or ground - 'destroying'. It is the pollution of the planetary surface, which includes the seas and the atmosphere. Just one of the techniques in the forefront of this agenda is deforestation.

"It is hard to imagine that this country of England, was, just a few hundred years ago almost entirely forested. Indeed so was most of Europe. The construction of wooden ships for the Navies of countries to expand their military, trade and industrial Empires was, in large part, responsible for this initially; because when you consider that it took around two thousand mature oak trees to construct just one warship, you can start to appreciate where they all went!

"Modern weaponry, due to the billions and billions spent on its research and development, is now capable of destroying – and does! - vast tracts of land unimaginably rapidly. Indeed the existing nuclear arsenals are more than capable of destroying the planet's surface many times over…and at the same time massively reducing the number of human inhabitants on it as well of course…

"That is their goal, to re-form, occupy, populate and truly have their dominion over this planet, retaining only a small number of humans to breed as livestock slaves, indeed, at that stage, by then, they would have...have destroyed, culled, killed, most – about ninety percent, of your race...and that process of their depopulation agenda is already well advanced...In fact it is actually 'written in stone', in many languages, carved into the huge monoliths of 'The Georgia Guide Stones', which mysteriously appeared in the late nineteen seventies, and are protected by The American Deep State. Please do your own research into them.

"The parasites have manipulated your race and your planet to be *almost* the complete opposites to what you and it were compared to long, long ago...*to what you and it really, truly, once were...*

"AND WILL BE SO AGAIN!" He said, raising his voice, his hands outstretched in front of him quivering as if they were about to receive a precious gift.

"How? How can that be even remotely possible now? – isn't

it just...too...late?" His voice had lowered to just above a whisper as he rhetorically asked that, but he now raised it up again. "Well, *it is possible, and it is Not Too Late!* Because despite all of the desperate attempts by the parasites to prevent it, more and more people are being 'kick started' to fire up again, due in great part to the tidal wave of positivity enhancing cosmic energies causing a raising of awakening to higher consciousness as they flow amongst you, en masse, all over this planet.

"As a result of this more and more people everyday are now 'waking up', and they are starting to consciously recognize those 'positive event dots' that I talked about before, to see them for what they really are...and that they are not just 'random coincidences' – and from there, your awareness, your consciousness and your perception will grow and grow – like the spreading cracks in a dam wall – *until finally that dam holding you back will burst open!* Because as more and more humans re-connect with their true perception, the realisation and knowledge of their true selves, and help and support each other by sharing, by reaching out with their expanding and connecting consciousness awareness, it is then you, each individual, each individual immensely powerful one of you who will be re-creating and re-energising the higher, positive frequencies of the global energy network - that have been all but decommissioned by the parasites.

"As well as being aware of the *'positive event dots'* - you will become aware of and see the real reason *for* and the real purpose of *why* there are so many *negative event dots* that happen time and time again, all over the world. And why the mainstream media focuses on and hypes them all up so much, bombarding you with graphic twenty four hour 'news' coverage of them just about everywhere you go. Everywhere you go because the television screen spewing all of this out at you is no longer just found in a private corner of your living room at home - and it wasn't so very long ago when it wasn't in nearly *every home*, but now it is, and as I say, and I'm sure you're all well aware that it's now just about everywhere you go out in the public arena. That is by design of course - so you are constantly exposed to it..."

Anders paused to take a quick sip of his water. He then cleared his throat, and started to talk again.

"A lady I spoke with last night at the Fair, just after my talk, and who I see is sat amongst us again now...," he nodded, with a smile, towards a middle-aged lady with a friend who were sat near to Sophie and Jake, "...and who I'm sure wouldn't mind me repeating for everyone some of what you were saying about all of this...?" The lady smiled whilst nodding back to him and pushing her hands forward for him to carry on.

"Thank you my dear, I would only ever repeat publicly, something said to me privately, with that person's permission of course. Last night you said to me, *'I'm free of it now, I no longer watch it, because I realised it was just constantly sapping and draining away my energy...for years I was addicted to it, and I really did use to feel drained by it at the end of a day - but now I feel so much better without it!'*.

"She said as well that it had been difficult at first, more difficult even than when she gave up drinking the drug alcohol, but what helped her through the withdrawal stages, in the early days of no television, was thinking of, and then making a weekly list of all the alternative, creative things she could do in the many hours that abstinence from it freed her to do instead!

Try doing all that yourselves, after even just a few days I've no doubts at all that you'll be feeling remarkably different – in a very positive way…!

He reached for his glass of water again and after taking a sip he grinned and turned his head over his shoulder to ask Alfie,

"I don't think you'll be putting one in here will you ol'chap?"

"*Certainly Not Mr. S!* This is, an' always will be a telly-free zone! In 'ere it's for folk to be *actually talkin' to each other* - an' listenin' to music - not sittin' goggle-eyed in a trance tekin' in loads o' that nonsense for hours on end!"

"Quite right! - And may it ever be so!" He chuckled and turned back to his audience.

"Let's have a look at some of those 'negative event dots' all around you. They are the constant and deliberately orchestrated wars, the so called 'terrorist atrocities', the corrupting of and the engineered dismantling and breakdown of living in what should be pleasant, harmonious societies. The financial crashes, and the ongoing pollution and destruction - of you and your planet. As you become more awake and aware, freeing your minds from the programming, and take a step back to see the bigger picture, you will realise as well that it is *mainly because of all those – and many more of course - negative event dots*, that contribute heavily to so many of you living now in an underlying state of deliberately engendered fear and deep anxiety. All those reoccurring, repeated events blasted out at you and reported on 'The T.V. News', and in the mainstream media. That state they get you into is the constantly reoccurring, repeated *First Stage* of an ongoing process called: the 'Hegelian Dialect', so named after the German philosopher Hegel who studied and explained the phenomena.

" *'The What?!' - 'Sounds a bit high-brow?!'* You may well be thinking! Well, put more simply it just means: 'Problem-Reaction-Solution'.

"That First Stage is to create the problem, 'the negative event dot' - so the public, the masses, react predictably by demanding that *'something must be done!'*, and that is the Second Stage, the stage of 'Reaction'. The Third Stage is 'Solution', which the controlling authorities have had ready to roll out all along, because they are manipulating and controlling every stage of this process. The Third Stage of course is more and more intrusion into your lives, more control over you, more and more power to a centralised global command and control system over all humanity. A humanity that has been deliberately programmed, entranced, and manipulated to willingly accept it.

"It can be so frustrating when you hear people whom are unaware of all this say: *'well – if you've not done anything wrong - what have you got to worry about? It's only to protect us! So what's the problem?'*.

"Well...they aren't the first to say that...it was Hitler's Minister for Propaganda, Josef Goebbels, who constantly repeated those, or very similar words, to justify everything the Nazi State was constructing...He also said: *'...if you are going to tell a lie – make it a big one! - And keep telling it – the people will soon believe it...!'*

An upto date example for you of that mindset, of, well, I call it 'programmed compliance', was given to me by a chap who spoke to me after one of my talks a few weeks ago in a city in the west of this country.

"I'm sure you will all recall the horrendous incident at the Manchester Arena when a young man detonated a bomb killing other young people who had gone to a music concert there. When the venue eventually reopened, the chap who spoke to me said he went with his wife to the first concert since the incident. This chap then told me they had to go through airport type body scanners, his wife's handbag was searched, and they were ordered around and herded like sheep by really intimidating looking security guards with aggressive attitudes – *'they looked like 'robo-cops' strutting around'*, he said, *'they were all dressed in black combat gear, with body armour, and some of them in the background, even wore black balaclavas hiding their faces...'*

"When he heard a young couple in front of him say to these 'robo-cops' as he described them, *'Thank you all for keeping us safe....!'* He told me – now remember these are all his words not mine! - He told me: *'I felt like throwing up! Couldn't these kids see what was really happening?! I just had to say to 'em: so you're alright with all of this are you then? - Well...they turned round and looked at me like I had two heads and hadn't had a bath for twelve months!'*

"I'm afraid I added to his consternation when I told him that the young bomber's father had been paid over forty thousand pounds by the British Security Services to assassinate Colonel Gaddaffi, the Libyan leader in the nineties, a plot that obviously failed, so the family clearly had a track record of being involved in 'Black Ops' – Black Operations - with the Security Services. Also the Imams at the young man's mosque had been so concerned about his extremist views that they had advised the local Police about him – but the Police took no action based on their concerns. One can't help but wonder where the: *'no action to be taken'* directive came from...Maybe if they *had* made some enquiries...?"

Anders inhaled a deep breath and let it out as a long sigh.

"Perhaps some of you may find all of this difficult to believe, or to even 'take on board', and certainly those whom are far less awakened, out there in the world at large *certainly will!* So let me introduce you now to just one of the male architects of all these types of negative events, and in a few minutes I'll mention another, a female one. I'll quote to you first some of *his own words about it all.* His name is, or was, as he died recently, Zbigniew Brzezinski. Officially he was the American President Jimmy Carter's National Security Advisor in the nineteen seventies. Unofficially he was a leading member of the elite's global cabal of master manipulators and architects of geopolitics. He said this over thirty years ago:

'...the public will shortly be unable to think or reason for themselves, they'll only be able to parrot the information they've been given on the previous night's television news...They will come to expect the media to do all their thinking and reasoning for them...The Technotronic Era is the gradual appearance of a more controlled society, dominated by an elite free from traditional values, and they will influence and control the people...'

"Note he said *'...free from traditional values...'*, I would suggest that those *'traditional values'* are: care, compassion, concern, empathy and love for your fellow humans, animals and the natural world. The opposite, being 'free' from them is the classic make-up of a psychopath..."

Anders shook his head, and sighed deeply again, pausing for a few moments to let all of this sink in to his audience. He then continued.

"As part of this agenda your bodies and minds are also attacked, weakened and changed by the poisoned food you eat, the poisoned water you drink, and the very air you breathe due to all the highly toxic substances they spray into it from aeroplanes - all are deliberately contaminated and poisoned. Your minds are even further attacked and changed by the poisonous, dangerous radiations you are now being surrounded with from all the addictive mobile communications technology devices being ever rapidly rolled out more and more across the planet. The ultimate goal of all that addictive technology – *Brzezinski's 'Technotronic Era'* - is to integrate, to fuse the human mind, the human consciousness, into a hive mind, that can be controlled by artificial intelligence, operated from a central global command, by those elites whom are the architects of all of this. As Brzezinski said: *'dominated by an elite...they will influence and control the people...'*

"Incidentally, and I don't want to stray too far, but this is worth mentioning, he was heavily involved in orchestrating events so the Russians invaded Afghanistan, in the late seventies, giving them what he described as: *'their Vietnam...'*. And that tragic war in Vietnam that America was lead by the nose into was started on spurious, false, and highly exaggerated events that were claimed to have happened by the elite architects in the Intelligence Services in a place called the Bay Of Tonkin, close to Vietnam, research it for yourselves, the information is all out there now.

"One of the longer term 'spin offs' from the Afghan war was the recruiting, training, funding and controlling of the Mujahadeen, which morphed after that war into the creation of proxy armies, under different names - Al Queda, Isis, etcetera, for the elite architects to use in theatres of wars in later years – now – in the Middle East – and all over the world of course. These elite architects plan decades ahead...

"...Those *'Manipulative Institutions'* I mentioned – such as divisive religions, the totally controlled and negatively mind programming corporate mainstream 'false news' media, the whole banking and money system, the ever invasive 'authorities' and so many, many, many others, all those 'negative event dots' that stem from them...all those negative events happening all around you...as you awaken you will begin to realise that they do not just exist or occur – *randomly or by chance – but by design...*

"...So you will start, as you begin to lift away those dimming veils of illusion, you will start to see how and why they all connect...and what the picture and the reality they reveal actually is, and what its real purpose actually is...and what lies - pun intended - behind it all...

"- And what lies behind it all of course is the creation of foul, evil, and ever abundant negative energies for the parasites' sustenance, and the currently gradual – but if they have their way, it will soon be not so gradual - depopulation of the planet...before they come in and claim it!

"...All those negative energy outpourings are vital sustenance for these evil parasitic energy vampires, and the creation of a lower global negative energy frequency here *on* your earth is being done, as I've said, and I'm repeating myself to emphasise the point, so that they can finally usurp humanity to colonise and physically exist *in* and *on* it...*fully claiming it as their domain...*

"...As you become more and more aware of all this you will realise that it has been *you* all along – *totally unwittingly of course, creating it for them* – so when you start to become aware again, you can then start to take back your conscious control of that ability, and create positive event dots, and start the repairing and the healing process...and then their, their house of foul cards will collapse...

"...It will not be effective to just simply treat, to address the symptoms – which are all those negative event dots that manifest, by demonstrating, by protesting, or by violent opposition - *because all that creates is more of what they want!* – A smorgasbord of *dis*-cord, *dis*-harmony, *dis*-ease, of anger and hate...*because all of those just create more and more powerful negative energies...!*

"...So...how do you start the repairing and healing process then...? If doing all that is not effective? But is actually *counter-productive?* Well, let me give you another analogy to answer that question: − doing all that protesting is just like shouting at a film or 'The News' you are watching on television or a large movie screen, *shouting at it will not change in the slightest what is happening on those screens!* - Instead You need to change what is being broadcast onto the screens *in the first place!* You need to change the actual reel of film...You need to get out of the passive and entranced audience and get back into the projection room, remove the vile film reel, replace it, *and start to broadcast , to transmit, your own! Your own individual reel of higher consciousness perception, and of understanding - because peace cannot be attained through violence, it can only be attained through understanding!*

"I don't claim the authorship of those last few words about 'understanding', they were actually said first by Einstein...But I certainly claim their veracity...because if *you* understand that *you* have to start to change *yourself* − *it is you* who starts to change - *The World.*

"...But, but, but...not every human in that audience, on this planet, is ready to de-trance, to awaken, to understand and help others to as well – *remember what I told you about 'Plato's Cave'?* - Some, many perhaps, will simply not be ready to understand, they will not be interested, some will refuse to even try to, some will fight tooth and nail to hold onto what they currently believe is 'the real world', some will go so far, give up, and then just carry on as they always have done...

Some will be so vehemently against it despite any and all of the facts that you can put in front of them, *some will even actively work against you and put all their misguided energies into ridiculing and discrediting such understanding - and try to discredit you personally as well...!*

"I quoted Einstein to you a few moments ago, well, something else that he said so insightfully about all of this was: *'...the world is a dangerous place – not so much because of those who do evil – but because of those who look on - and do nothing about it..."*

"SO WHY? Why would people behave like that?! - Well, one reason is because it threatens the very core, the very fabric of the only reality, and self identity that they have been programmed to believe in...So, there will, sadly, always be those you just cannot reach whilst they are in that...in that current stage of their development...

"...Which brings us now to another part of the reason, the answer to: 'WHY, why would they do that?'...Well, now we come to the others, in all walks of life, but mainly concentrated in the so called 'Elites' in the upper levels of the pyramids of the hegemonic and hierarchical power structures of the Manipulative Institutions that are currently in place on this planet. In those upper levels are *those – like Brzezinski was – those who know exactly what is happening...because they are complicit in it, they are playing an active role in it,* as willing agents of the predatory parasitic energy vampires and their evil, dark agenda...

"...WHY ? Why? Why would they do that? - Well, it's really quite simple! - *Because they are being very well rewarded during their physical lives here for doing so...!*

"...They are chosen to occupy elite positions in the manipulative institutions because they are also naturally inclined to negativity, and to psychopathy, which is a complete lack of empathy, care or compassion towards others, and they have a burning desire to manipulate and control people for their own ends, and to them, those ends will always justify the means.

"An example of this in action was an interview some of you may recall, it was just a few years ago, it was, very surprisingly, actually on a mainstream media television broadcast. So now I want to introduce you to the second, as I mentioned a few minutes ago, female this time, 'architect' – I'm only mentioning two for now – but there are many, many more involved in all of all this.

"The interviewer asked Marie Korbelova - who was born in Czechoslovakia, but in later years became an American citizen called Madeleine Albright, and she became the American Secretary of State in the Clinton administration. She was asked in the televised interview if she thought that the deaths, the killing, of half a million children in Iraq was justified to achieve the military aims of the coalition forces...she replied unhesitatingly: '...*Yes, I think It Was....*'

"Half a million! — five...hundred...thousand...little children...killed! And how many tens of thousands more were grievously wounded, maimed for life? And both she and many others in the system she served thought that killing and maiming them all was... 'justified'..."

Anders gasped in absolute dismay, visibly affected again by saying this, and sipped at his water for a moment, his hands trembling. Slowly replacing the glass, he took a deep breath and continued talking.

"Or, if they are not naturally inclined to be so, these people are made to have psychopathic traits by the insidious use of what is called: 'trauma based mind control techniques'. This is done to them from a very young age – I won't shock you all by going into the specific details about that now, but just to give you *some idea* of what it entails - one part of that process includes the selected children of the elites, and not just the elites, to watch and then participate in the torturing, killing and butchering of animals, animals at first...then of people, including other children...Testimonies from those who managed, in their later years, despite all the odds of them doing so, who managed to break out and escape from these wicked programmes verify all these, and many more of the obscene details...

"I'll say it again: *these elite psychopaths are people whom have absolutely no empathy, care or compassion whatsoever for the suffering, pain, misery and anguish of others...*They are an entirely different and despicably aberrant species of human.

"Now...most 'normal' humans would possibly reply to all of those statements by saying: *'Oh No, No, No – All that's Ridiculous! - Fantasy! - That Doesn't Happen! Can't be! - They Wouldn't Do That...!'*

"...My reply to them when they say that is: *'No - of course You Can't Believe or envisage that there are people whom are capable of being so evilly callous - and whom do a thousand more other, just as heinous things! - Because You Wouldn't Do It! Because you are a normal and a decent human being! It is too far beyond anything you can perceive! But the truth is though, that They Do...! And they do it all the time!'"*

Anders then raised an arm in a friendly gesture towards Jake, whilst sipping again at his water, and said, "which, hopefully, by now, has more than started to approach the answer to your question..? - But I will come back to it again in more detail before I finish – to specifically what and who you saw following you tonight, and what dangers, what threats to you they pose – *and what you, all of you, can do about countering it and them* - is that okay with you...?"

Jake, shocked, and deep in thought, nodded his head slowly in agreement, Sophie noticed others doing the same. She herself felt deeply shocked as well, blitzed by all of this, all at once, as well as saddened, and dismayed, and she was sure everyone else must be feeling the same too. She felt as well that all of what Anders was saying – because it was such a big, sudden and *very unsettling* 'info drop', that it would take her some time to absorb and fully get her head around it and process it all...but...it was already answering many of her own questions that she'd had for a long time now about so many of the terrible things going on in the world...shown in the newspapers and on the television's 'News'...

Last night at the Fair Anders had talked much more generally, a sort of entry level introduction about all of these things and to a much larger audience than tonight, but even that more diluted, introductory, general version had started to change everything for her, but now, tonight, with this new, and more detailed input she could almost feel previously unused parts of her brain responding by firing up and sending signals down long dormant neural pathways, and starting to clear away all the accumulated cobwebs. Ha! - Not 'The Windmills Of Your Mind' like the song played loudly earlier on the merry-go-round, but 'The Cobwebs Of Your Mind!' Despite the lingering shock and sadness her mind rallied, to counter and attempt to dispel it by chuckling out loudly to herself, and on hearing her Jake quizzically tilted his head closer to hers, and even with his feelings of being shocked and downbeat himself, it was with a grin and an amused and quiet whisper that he asked her, "what y'chucklin' away at...?!"

Sophie, slightly embarrassed and hoping no-one else had

114

heard her, pressed her lips tightly together whilst lowering her head, her eyes wide as she raised her shoulders looking like a naughty school girl caught out for talking in class, then she pouted her lips as she whispered "Ssssh! He's talking…!"

Jake, still grinning at her, whispered back in mock admonishment, "Pay Attention you naughty girl!" She quickly put her tongue out at him, then smiled widely, pushing herself affectionately closer to him, and looked over to Anders, ready to listen intently again.

"…and as you do…when you really start to see through and understand all of the imposed, programmed false illusions, and say so to others, and try to point them out to others, as your growing perception clears away the veils of illusion *on* this world, and lets that brilliant light from the lamp, *which never stopped shining,* back in, you will feel that it is only natural, as a normal and decent human being to try to connect to others to help them to awaken. Because as decent normal human beings your truly *natural inclinations* are to love, help and care for others, to empathise, and to show compassion. To help them, and by doing so you will be helping yourself…because always remember: *Love is the Most Powerful Of All The Energies,* and Love is the only thing you can keep and grow...*by giving it away...*"

Anders paused again, then gave out a sour chuckle. "But, as I have said, helping others to awaken is much easier said than done...because a frustratingly curious thing about so many humans is that they can be shown, so then they can observe, the truth all around them, but so often they cannot tolerate its implications, so they blind themselves to it. They shut it off from their senses, and put it out of their minds, just to avoid the facts that glaringly contradict their own interpretation of the world.

"I remember, Ha! Ha! I remember Winston saying about all of this at a meeting we had once..."

He pointed at a black and white photo' over on the wall, it was the classic pose of Winston Churchill glowering at the viewer.

"Winston said: '...*when a man, on occasion, stumbles over*

the truth, more often than not he quickly picks himself up, dusts himself down, and then scuttles away as if nothing had happened!'"

This statement, and then Ander's expression of pantomimed surprise as he acted out brushing himself down, and scuttling away, taking a few rapid steps along the coffee bar, caused several people in the room to chuckle in light relief. Smiling, he returned with normal gait back to the counter. Pleased at the result of this little display of humour, which is always such a big and powerful antidote to distress...he thought that perhaps a little more of it might be appropriate...

"Actually you know, that photograph, iconic as it is and so familiar to just about everybody, isn't quite what it appears to be either...because...whilst the photographer Yousuf Karsh was setting up his equipment for that portrait session Winston was jovial, relaxed and smiling a lot. But on that occasion Yousuf didn't want a photograph portraying Winston like that, that friendly and relaxed aspect of him, no no no - instead he wanted one showing a stern, powerful and authoritative image of Winston then in nineteen forty one as a Leader Of A Nation

At War!

"So...without telling him when he was all ready to start clicking away with his camera – and in complete surprise, with no warning, Yousuf quickly reached over and snatched out the large cigar Winston had in his mouth – and immediately took that photo' using a long cable release concealed in his other hand! Winston's immediate reaction to the effrontery of Yousuf doing that, was his stern facial expression and imposing bodily posture that you can see! Seconds later Winston burst out laughing as he realised what the photographer had done! Very clever eh?! Anyway....!"

This tale caused actual laughter, not just a few chuckles in the room. Sophie's and Jake's included, and Sophie couldn't help thinking that Anders was describing events that happened, what, nearly eighty years ago! - As if he had been there to witness them...? No, surely not...?!

"Right, well, where was I...?" Anders asked also laughing lightly. "Oh yes...your awakening perception and conscious awareness that things, in fact almost everything in your society, is deliberately created to be inverted, *and just not right*, and is not by any means how it should really, naturally be. And an awareness that you have been deliberately locked down into a limiting mere five senses, and why and how, and what is behind all of that, hidden in the shadows. That awareness and understanding will not be an easy task to convey to others who are as yet unaware...and, sadly, just about impossible with some...Nevertheless, it is a crucial and Noble Quest for you to embark upon...because at its heart is literally the future of your race and your planet for aeons to come..."

Anders paused again, and took another sip of water. Alfie, noting it was now nearly empty quickly put another full glass down for him.

"Oh, thank you Alfie – Actually I'm not too far off from being finished for this evening - and then I'll enjoy one of your excellent coffees – and maybe even one or two of those delicious looking chocolate biscuits that I spied when I was scuttling away just now!"

"O'course Mr. S.! The missus made 'em – thems y'like - special for yer she did - thought y'might! Whenever yer

ready!" Alfie said. Having thanked Alfie, he turned back to the room.

"As you all just heard – and I don't mean my...my weakness for Alfie's good lady's excellent chocolate biscuits...! But that I've nearly finished for this evening – now I know *I've put rather a lot of information, and some of it, with no doubt, is quite shocking,* in front of you all at once, and I'm very grateful to you all for your patience in listening to me...

"...Now – as I was talking about cameras and film before - has anyone here seen the movie film made in nineteen eighty nine called: "They Live' ?" About half of the audience let him know that they had.

"Oh good! Those of you who haven't – I strongly recommend it to you! My friend Ray Nelson who was the author of the original book, which was called 'Eight O'clock In The Morning', he wrote it years before the film was made, back in sixty three. He was delighted when it was made into quite an excellent film by John Carpenter. Well, I think the film version was more of a documentary really with what it very effectively puts across! It is definitely worth watching, and was quite ahead of it's time. There's a scene in it - that I'll describe briefly now, which cleverly illustrates what Ray knew about what I've said about communicating 'all of this' to others.

"– Right, this is it - the main character had earlier in the film found a box full of sunglasses, which, when he put a pair of them on they enabled him to see the world as it really was - and was not at all dissimilar to what I have described...well, in this particular scene he tries to get his new friend to put a pair on after he's described to him what they enabled him to see...but his friend refuses to! So they argue and end up having a humdinger of a fight! - One of the longest fight scenes ever in a film at the time! - Fists flying, rolling around the floor, the whole shebang!

"...Anyway, at the end of the fight his friend does actually put them on...and he instantly sees the world around him for what it really is...and he's struck dumb with the shock! If I remember it correctly he falls down on his backside due to that shock! And from then on he allies with the main character and they...*well, I won't spoil it for those of you yet to watch it!* The point is, is that long fight scene was simply a clever cinematic allegory for the difficulty one can face in convincing or getting people, *even a friend...to do something – and to see...*"

A man in the audience then responded by humorously asking out loud, "I'm all for trying to help people 'to see' – as long as I'm not going to have to get into a fistfight and roll around the floor every time someone refuses to...*I don't think I'd last the day out?!*"

Everyone laughed, the atmosphere now much lightened, Anders also laughed and then said, "Goodness me no! *Certainly not!* - The negative energy of violence is exactly what they want you to create! This has to be a totally non-violent revolution! Remember what Einstein said about Attaining Peace? And look at what Gandhi achieved against the full might of the British Empire by doing just that! And what, what was it he said – oh yes... *'At first they will ignore you, then they will ridicule you, then they will fight you, and then you will...Win...!'*" Several people clapped and quietly cheered.

"...But the secret is, and this is what the parasitic predators are really afraid of, and are now at this time desperately throwing everything they can at your race to prevent this from happening. The secret is, is that if only a modest percentage of humans on this planet awaken, that will be enough to become a tipping point to start to make *Your World* a very different place to what it has become, as the healing and repairing process will take firm hold. Because those awakened people will automatically be connecting their consciousnesses to create an unstoppably powerful force. Then, if, and when, you humans understand what and who you really are - you would be impossible for the parasites and their elite minions in the manipulative institutions to control – and the low, negative frequency dwelling parasitic predatory vampires cannot survive for long in such an environment, an environment of much higher positive frequencies, the frequencies emitted from caring, from compassion, from Love, the highest frequency of them all...

"Actually, the phenomena – of just a few members of a species learning 'how to do' something and then soon all of that species knowing 'how to do it' baffles and challenges the paradigms of mainstream establishment science. The phenomena is called *'The Hundredth Monkey Syndrome'*...

"I'll briefly explain it for you: a group of monkeys on one island were taught and trained how to perform a simple task, with food as a reward. Then, after something in the region of a hundred or so of them learned how to do it, what amazed the scientists was that after that number was achieved - *all the monkeys on the island knew how to do it!* And not just on that island but on the mainland as well – where they had had no physical contact! Then they discovered that all the monkeys of that species *across the whole World...also knew how to do it!* This is just one example of the evidence of a collective connecting consciousness in a species, *where the knowledge and the ability to do something can be accessed automatically, and or, at will, by any one of them - as and when they desire to.*

"So of course traditional mainstream establishment science – one of those 'Manipulative Institutions' - has a big problem with that! Because in their world view they have to explain everything only in terms of what the limited, *materialistic* five senses can see and touch, etcetera, so they can weigh, measure and repeat it in a laboratory. Empirical science they call it, Empty science I call it...

"But the masses have been programmed for so long to believe and to be in awe of these scientific authority figures because they are called *'experts'* – *so what they are saying must be right!*

"It's rather like the priests of old who said only they knew The Truth! So any scientist 'going public' and giving explanations for such phenomena beyond the officially sanctioned, limited range of *'solid-and-separate-reality-is-all-there-is'* paradigm and parameters, will soon find their funding cut off, their careers – even their lives - at risk, whilst being pursued by the hunting-hound-like-baying of ridicule from their sceptically indoctrinated, narrow minded peers…

"Einstein said on this very issue: *'Great spirits have always found violent opposition from mediocrities. The latter cannot understand it when a man does not thoughtlessly submit to hereditary prejudices – but honestly and courageously uses his intelligence…'*

"Having said all that though there are now many who are openly and bravely researching the phenomena of the unseen and managing to get their work out into the World, into your collective consciousness, despite the barrage of mainstream corporate media's scepticism and ridiculing...when they are not totally ignoring it. Those doing this re-pioneering work is in tune with what Nikola Tesla phrased so perfectly a hundred years or so ago when he said: *'...if you want to find the secrets of the universe, think in terms of energy, frequency and vibration...'* How so very right he was – and look what happened, tragically to him...How different your world would be today if his works and discoveries about harnessing 'Free Energy for everyone' had been implemented...

"Well...to return briefly to the actual parasites again...they managed to survive when they first arrived here – aeons ago – mainly because there were so few humans on the planet then than compared to today, and they quickly ambushed and controlled a totally unsuspecting and naively trusting race. It is a military truism that: *'the well planned offence will overcome an unplanned defence, every time...'*

"...But these predators and their cabal of 'elite minions' are now absolutely minuscule in number compared to the amount of humans on the planet today. *And it is all of you who have the real power, not them!* And more and more of you, every passing day now, are becoming aware of exactly that, and so the control over you that they so desperately need - is weakening...

"...So even if only a small percentage of humans fully awaken at first, as they do so they will each automatically be raising the levels of their own individual, conscious, positive energy manifestation creating transmissions, and so positively be impacting on the whole human collective consciousness. *Because we are all consciously connected energetically* – yes you are separate *physical* entities on this planet to experience this third dimension, yes - but your *true self* is an immortal spiritual being, you are all part of one great consciousness. All of you are like divine sparks from an eternal fire – or like individual drops of water that all together make up just one great, and ever present ocean.

"That has been one of the key deceptions and hidden from you all along – that the positive, deliberate creations and manifestations from your individual and collective positive energy transmissions will grow exponentially and re-energise the planetary grid. And, as I have said, that will be enough to create a raising of the planet's energy frequency environment within which the parasites cannot survive in – let alone operate in. And so, when they've finally gone...your race will be free to soar again...

"...So that is what they really fear, and that is what is really happening now...and it is happening synchronistically with other cyclic waves of positive energies starting to reach the Earth now from the far reaches of the Cosmos...It is one reason why in very recent years there have been so many revelations from those previously in the power elites, or those still in them and close to and aware of what is being done to you. Why? Well, it's because they can see the great changes that are about to come, and are jumping ship, always remember - *'it is the little straws that tell you which way the big wind is blowing...'*

"I'll talk more, or another of us will, about all this in more detail another time, and the fact that your Earth is a Living, Sentient, Female Entity. Actually, in HP Lovecraft's excellent book, he wrote it in the seventies, he called it 'Gaia', he goes into this concept in great detail, perhaps you'll read it if you haven't already!

"Oh Dear! I am sorry! I'm starting to sound like an old Headmaster giving out lots of homework to you all! - A short story about Plato's Cave to read, a film to watch! Books to read! Tasks to perform! It's nice homework though! – Not that any school I know of *on* Earth currently teaches any of this, of course...!"

Everyone laughed. "Actually, above all, what I really want you to do - is to do your own research, because I am not standing here *telling you what you must believe!* - The World is full of Individuals and Institutions, as I've said, already doing that! And most of them are doing so with the intentions and agendas that I've described. No...I'm not doing that at all, all I can do is present this to you, and it is then upto you, to your own free will to make of it what you want, I am not a Guru, a Preacher or a Prophet, I am just, just someone who is from a, a movement that wants to help your race to achieve that tipping point at this exciting time of your race's unfolding story...of your evolution...of your re-awakening...That Awaits You All."

Spontaneous clapping and some whistling approval erupted, Sophie and Jake joining in with it. Everyone in the room all felt again that feeling of immense power and gentle goodness tangibly radiating out from Anders. Sophie thought to herself that Anders was being incredibly humble and over modest because...because he is so obviously much more than he appears or seems to be. He just seems, and a strange thought came to her...so 'otherworldly', and so does Maria, and that old Gypsy lady Magda Leah Rose - now *she* was definitely more than she seemed...she was *so* 'otherworldly'!...And with everything that has happened already this evening...was that so beyond 'belief'? But it *had* all happened, and with everything she'd heard just now, well, maybe that's not so strange to think, maybe he, and they, are...

Anders had raised his palms in humility and gratitude towards everyone. "Thank you all! Thank you!" He said as they quietened down.

"Following on from when I said: *'not telling people what they must believe...'*, but instead, perhaps, gently nudging them towards considering things they haven't been aware of before –

try this: when you get a suitable opportunity, let's say you're chatting with people in a social setting, one way to start to approach all of this is, for example, just to start things off, say something along the lines of: *'I read something fascinating the other day – what do you think about it? - The article I read said that...'*, and then proceed to say – well, paraphrase it all of course! - It doesn't have to be word for word!...:

"...If all the currently known multiple energy frequencies in this Universe, from the lowest wavelengths to the highest were, for the sake of this example, able to be covered by a ruler one metre long, well, the electro magnetic frequency of visible light – that is the spectrum of light that is visible to our current human ability to decode it into seeing 'things' - would cover *significantly less than five millimetres* of that ruler *a thousand millimetres long*! Less than a mere five millimetres! And that fact is actually verified by our so called 'mainstream science'. So there's no wonder that the majority of us humans currently – don't decode, see or understand very much at all! Because we're almost blind to everything *that is really out there!*

"Try it, I'm not saying it will work everytime of course! But you will, hopefully, sometimes find that it can work as an entrée, an opening, to expand and continue into other areas of...further interesting, and related discussion topics...

"Because you are initially stating verifiable facts - not subjective opinions or personal suppositions, you are more likely to avoid what is called in logical argument, or logical debate, an *'ad hominem'* verbal attack. The phrase is Latin, and basically means: 'against the man'. That is when the listener verbally disparages aspects of your character, and, or, you as a person, even your appearance, to avoid confronting, or even acknowledging the issue you are introducing...'ad hominem' can very effectively serve to deliberately and calculatingly distract others *from even considering what you are saying*...the mainstream media use this technique constantly of course – usually with gross and false exaggerations – because it influences people not to listen or consider valid what the targeted person *is actually saying – often with factual proofs..!*

"Putting 'ad hominem' to one-side - although before we do I must say that reading up about *all the fallacious techniques* people use in logical arguments to dispute you would be a useful and rewarding thing to do, and then listen to Politicians using them as well, *because they are masters of them!* Oh! Sorry! That's More 'Homework!' - It's sad to say, but you will still encounter all the programmed, knee jerk responses of denial and disinterest of anything beyond the individual bubbles of limited mindset preoccupations *that so many people live still within, and are enveloped by though ... "*

Anders waved his arms up in the air, then let them slap down to his sides, his posture slumped, and he emitted a baleful sigh. He turned slightly, reaching for the glass of water again, and took a long draught from it. Then, pausing as he dabbed at his lips with a large white handkerchief which he had flourished from his breast pocket, he carefully folded and replaced it, then stood up ramrod straight, shoulders back, legs apart, hands on hips and said...

"But Things *Are* Changing!- Those enveloping bubbles of limited mental preoccupations *are* being 'popped'! - Imagine a tennis ball in someone's hand being held down in the dregs at the bottom of a deep bucket full of dirty water, but the grip on that ball is weakening, and when it finally releases its hold that ball will quickly surge upwards to the surface, where its true natural place is. Or, imagine a helium filled balloon held down onto the ground in a grey stormy landscape - suddenly it's released - and then it immediately surges up, up above the fog and the dark clouds blanketing the landscape, and into the truly bright blue sky and the infinite yonder! - Well, that tennis ball and that balloon represent the rising human consciousness and its attendant higher perceptions – *'popping up'!*"

He chuckled saying, "Actually, as analogies those two only go part way, because as your consciousness surges upwards it will rapidly re-expand, re-grow, and re-connect you to the light, to the knowing, and to the *understanding* of the infinite - all those remaining 'nine hundred and ninety five plus millimetres' that your physical brain cannot currently decode - but you get the idea!"

Sophie had a sudden flashback to lunchtime when she was sat on the bench by the harbour wall, looking up into the infinite blue sky...part of her...knowing...and almost readying itself to soar up and fly amongst the clouds and into the blue...just before Jake...by 'coincidence'...had spoken to her...and that had lead to…

"SO! Finally we come to who or what *specifically* are 'they' who were following you two earlier, and what danger did they represent?! He said, looking over towards Jake and Sophie.

"Actually – did anyone else here see or sense being watched or followed by anyone - they could have been male or female, of any age…?"

Most of the people sat in the room looked around at each other, shaking their heads, saying 'no's' and 'don't think so's…', but a youngish looking man with his girlfriend, sat partly out of sight to Sophie and Jake, hesitantly raised his hand, saying, "Well, I, I er, I think we did! Yes, well, I know we did…We'd both been here – well not, in here…!" He gestured around him, "but at the marquee, last night when we listened to you…and so we came again tonight, wanting to listen to you again, and we asked one of the lads at the merry-go-round where the marquee was - like everyone else that's here, well, those that we've spoken to did apparently. But, everyone in here arrived, well it seemed like one after the other, over a few minutes that's all, which I don't quite understand how, because...well, you'd've thought it would've taken ages for everyone to arrive..."

Anders answered him quickly, wanting to get him back onto the subject of the followers.

"That is just an effect of the time portal's operating system – we set it so that anyone entering – through that particular portal doorway, would seem to arrive only a minute or so after the previous person or persons had – despite how much time in the outside world had actually passed. Basically we recalibrated a reverse polarity of the space-time continuum, reversing it from the more usual time-space continuum as we didn't want to keep you all waiting for too long! But do forgive me for interrupting you – please carry on!"

Anders had explained this so rapidly and so matter of factly, it was as if he was simply explaining an everyday quite minor technical issue about some household appliance!

Jake nuzzled Sophie's ear again, whispering, "Well, we've

now gone from bein' in 'Tales O' The Unexpected' to 'The Twilight Zone', to definitely now bein' in a real life episode o' 'Dr. Who'!" Sophie blew her lips out in bemusement, shaking her head slightly, shrugging her shoulders.

"I don't mind though..." Jake said with a grin, "...*Dr. Who is one o'mi favourites...!*"

Sophie grinned, looking at him. *"Mine too! – And Star Trek!"* She whispered, a big smile on her face.

The young man who had been talking before was blinking rapidly, a vacant look on his face, as he was obviously struggling to process what Anders had just said, but his girlfriend leaned forward on their table to look over towards Sophie and Jake, giving them a little wave saying, "Hi there! We saw two middle aged men in dark clothes - bit like 'The Men In Black'! But without the dark sunglasses! - Were they like the ones who followed you two as well?"

Sophie leaned forwards as well saying, "Hi! Yeah, well, sort of, they weren't exactly the same but both had longish dark coats, I, I wouldn't normally've probably thought twice about them, but when I saw their eyes...*just staring at us...horrible black tar like evil eyes...it freaked me out!*"

"*Yeah!* – That's what, *what freaked us out a bit too!* Dave thought I was being paranoid or something at first!" She looked at the young man she was sat next to, "*Yes you did!* But then you saw them as well, didn't you?! - Then lots of other people wandered in front of them, and the two men had disappeared when they'd passed! *So, I dunno - but it was weird!*"

"Mmmm, from what you've both just said," Anders joined in, "I think they might have been what we call 'The Watchers', we call them that because that is the name the British Security Service MI5 calls their lower level surveillance agents. Let me explain...you remember I said earlier that there are networks of 'elite' humans who willingly act for, and are agents for implementing much of the parasite's dark agenda...? Those networks are permeated by all the secret societies the elites belong to. Well, The Watchers are on the much lower, 'street level' rungs of that network. Nowadays they tend to be people who are selected for having a degree of psychic ability combined with a, let's just say, either a pre-existing negative inclination, or they are...altered...to have one, they are then further corrupted and mind controlled, so they become utterly compliant and give themselves up to be employed and used, mainly as spies by the parasites...

"...I said *'nowadays'*, because they are not a modern day phenomena by any means...Just a few centuries ago, during the terrible, unbelievably evil and barbaric times of 'The Congregation Of The Holy Inquisition Of The Holy Office', or more commonly known as 'The Inquisition', operated by the so called 'Black Friars', which was an ecclesiastical tribunal set up by the Catholic Church in the twelve hundred and fifties, and it openly existed until the early eighteen hundreds. The institution still exists somewhat clandestinely however under the name of 'The Congregation For The Doctrine Of The Faith', and its role is still to defend the church against the 'danger' of new and unacceptable doctrines…

"Throughout all that time The Watchers would seek out, spy on, and pass information onto others higher up in the organisation who would then torture 'confessions of heresy' from the men, women and children they had targeted.

"Those poor unfortunates who managed to actually survive the incredibly hideous and barbaric tortures inflicted upon them - and those tortures were all sanctioned by that major 'manipulative institution': the Church - when those poor souls, in unbelievable agony, 'confessed', they were then handed over to The State for public execution...usually by being burnt alive...as 'The Holy Church' couldn't be publicly seen to have blood on its hands of course.

"Thousands of lay persons were recruited to form a vast network of Watcher spies all across Europe and beyond to seek out the so called heretics. The word 'heretic', comes from the Greek verb *'to choose'*, and basically meant a free-thinker, someone who wasn't in agreement with the Holy Catholic Church's Mind Control Doctrine, which encompassed and controlled a vast swathe of humanity. The Inquisition targeted Jews, Muslims, Protestants, the Gypsies and those of the Old Pagan Religions - and even people from the congregations of their own Catholic churches who had, or were accused of, contravening just one of the thirty or forty dictates *of acceptable thinking, speech and behaviour...*

"I remember clearly the words of the early Roman poet Titus Lucretius Carus, written many centuries previously, which rang never more true than during the terrible times of The Inquisition, he said: *'Tantum religio potuit suadere malorum'*...Which translates from the original Latin to:

'So potent a persuasion to evil is religion...'"

Anders then took several deep breaths, wringing his hands as he stared up at the ceiling, after a few moments he calmed himself and continued speaking. "Do forgive me, I have perhaps, digressed slightly, anyway...*back to the Watchers of 'nowadays'...!* In their case they are used as spies, like human surveillance cameras, as viewers of their surroundings, and particularly of people. Because of their psychic ability, and for other genetic reasons, the parasites can easily tune in and use them to – literally – see through their eyes...! What you saw in their eyes, that blackness, and why you felt like you did, was because you got a glimpse of that evil, intensely negative

141

energy looking out at you...The Watchers are more effective for longer term surveillance, and less, well, less detectable than the 'remote viewers' they also use are."

Everyone sitting in the Cafe was suddenly very silent and very still. Despite all the mind shaking revelations that Anders had previously spoken about, this was zeroing in to the right here, the right now. And it made the right here, right now, suddenly very real to them all.

"Just before I arrived I believe Maria briefly mentioned that the marquee had been moved because those opposed to what we are doing had found it...? Yes...?" Maria nodded in agreement.

"Well, having located the marquee - in the early hours of this morning - which was, is, by the way part of just one of the many camouflaged portals that Maria, myself and many others use...the parasites obviously then decided to send in Watchers to the Fair this evening for them to observe, to see, literally, who turned up again, but especially to identify those who did who now have their powerful psychic abilities re-awakening...prior to further steps then being taken against them by the parasites' acting through them. Now, at this point - let me just zoom out a little bit – to, as I've said before – to give you some more background to all this...

"...Maria and I, and many others like us, are constantly going all over your World to give presentations, guidance, and much, much more...to people like your very good-selves, who are now waking up. And, just like someone waking up in a strange bed, and perhaps in a room they don't quite recognise – it can be, shall we say - *a little disconcerting!* Which is when we, and others, can come in...to explain, to help, and to offer guidance – not to try and convince or convert you or anything like that – ultimately it is upto each of you as individuals to decide upon what you then choose to do, all we can do is reach out to you...

"...Now...at the moment, when you look at someone, you perhaps just see - that someone! But, in time, as your abilities develop further, you will be able to see that person's aura. We all have one! Part of it can even be photographed! Some special types of photographic film are sensitive to the higher frequencies of light than your brain cannot, at the moment, *decode and 'see'* – you remember me talking earlier about the 'less than only five millimetres'...?! It was an old Russian friend and colleague of mine, called Kirlian who first photographed them...'Kirlian Photography' of the aura was named after him.

"Well, through the Watchers' eyes the parasites can see the physical you of course - but they can also see your auras. And as awakening beings, and *especially* as awakening beings with emergent psychic abilities, your auras are much brighter, more multi-coloured, much more expanded, much bigger - than those of people whom haven't yet fully, or even started to become awaked. So if a small group of you who have awakened are drawn together the cumulative effect is like that of a lighthouse to the Watchers – *a beacon visible for miles!* So..."

"*...So they're like moths to a flame then...?!*" The same girl as before asked him.

"*Yes!* – That's the sort of idea." Anders replied.

"But unlike moths, the parasites, through the Watchers, will first identify, then *scan you*, to probe and see what psychic defences you have in place – if any...*before then sending in others we call 'The Wreckers'.* Now these beings have additional skills and a much greater degree of psychic prowess which the parasites will further amplify, to do their job, which is to, by various means – by using exotic technology as well as psychically – initially try to deal with you by focusing on disrupting your body's and mind's crucial electromagnetic energy circuits to...to cause a dampening down of your consciousness and aura, *to put it bluntly - to sabotage you.* If you have watched the Harry Potter films you will have seen the 'Dementas', wraith like spectral creatures sucking the life force out of their victims, well, what they are portrayed in those films as being capable of doing is similar to what the Wreckers can do. The main difference is that The Wreckers can do it to you at a distance. Because those of you whom have awakened, are, as I've said, a great threat of course to them now..."

He rubbed his chin, thinking deeply, and paced round in a small circle. "Mmm, but...*I wonder...*"

Stopping his pacing suddenly, he looked over to Maria and

asked her, "I say Maria, what do you think? - I'm just wondering if they have changed tactics? - I'm thinking that because these good people here described those they saw as being like 'The Men In Black', wearing dark clothes – which, for some reason, is classic Wrecker apparel, whereas the Watchers, well, as you know, they can be almost invisible because they look just like anyone else by wearing indistinguishable not-a-second-glance-at normal everyday clothes, and can be male or female of any age...so they can hide in plain sight...!"

Before Maria could reply to him he turned back to both the young couple, and to Sophie and Jake asking them, "- Did any of you feel slightly dizzy, tingly, or feel a sudden muzzy headache coming on - *that was a little bit enervating to start with at the time?!*"

"Yes! - I did!" Sophie said, even though she wasn't quite sure what 'enervating' meant.

"But, well, when Jake came back from chasing them off - even though he hadn't seen them, he, well, he, *ahem...he gave me a big hug and a kiss!* So then I felt great and not scared anymore and the dull, drainy migraine like feeling of a headache that had just started just sort of went! - *And I forgot about it -'til now!"* As she was saying this she blushed, slightly embarrassed!

"Huh! So did I! – But *I* didn't get *a big hug and a kiss!"* The other girl commented wryly, but with some amusement, pouting and pushing at her boyfriend – who then immediately gave her a one armed big hug and a loud smackerooney of a kiss on her cheek, and said, *"Better late than never then eh?!"*

The atmosphere in the room changed positively as everyone laughed.

"Excellent! *Excellent!"* Anders said, quietly clapping. He then addressed Sophie and Jake again. "It was obviously that sudden outpouring of the higher emotions of love and affection from you both that dispelled, literally dis-spelled the lower negative energies flowing into you from them! As I have said, it is the higher frequencies generated by those emotions that they cannot tolerate, penetrate or withstand..."

He then looked at the other young couple and said, "and I think what happened, fortunately for you two, was that as a large group of other people suddenly came between you and them, all those passing auras shielded you enough to give interference and cause a breaking off of the connection they were making to you..."

"But...how come they then just disappeared!? - *In a second or less!* Sophie exclaimed.

"Y-ees, it's, er, it's a, *a mite technical.*" Anders replied speaking slowly, thinking how best to explain it for her, and for all of them.

"Well...what they actually did was have the, the factors of their visible light reflection parameters quickly altered to a frequency that your sight could not decode – they were still there - but you just couldn't see them! It's similar to the sort of thing a good stage hypnotist can achieve – he or she can have someone stand right in front of a person they had...programmed...not to see...and they wouldn't! *That someone would be quite invisible to them – but not to anyone else present!*

"The parasites can only do that for a very small length of time however, just a few minutes at most, because it takes a tremendous amount of energy for them *to immediately implement and maintain,* but it's usually enough to allow them to escape away unseen. They tend to do that only when there are too many potential witnesses around...or if the human they are possessing is facing a physical threat that would...damage or disable that human...they are just, well, *protecting their assets in those cases...!*"

"Aye too right! - I'd've damaged an' disabled their assets alright if I'd caught 'em!" Jake interjected. *"Pickin' on Sophie an' givin' 'er a right scare like that...!"*

More, but subdued laughter came from those present as they glanced briefly over to Jake, seeing a large and powerfully built young man with long blondish hair wearing a black leather motorbike jacket and faded blue jeans. He definitely looked like an individual that they would not like to get on the wrong side of most of them thought!

"- My Hero aren't you! Rescuing me! - *A damsel in distress!*"
Sophie said to him with a wide grin.

"Well...*ah dunno abaht bein' an 'ero,* just did what any, well
most men woulda done like...!" Jake replied rather sheepishly,
and this time it was his turn to actually blush slightly and be a
little embarrassed!

Anders smiled and said, "*Well I think you are all Heroes!*
And as nobody has left – *or asked to leave anyway* – do I take
it that you all wish to stay...? You are absolutely quite free to
leave here of course if you so wish...! He looked around
seeing all their heads shaking, indicating that everyone
intended staying. "No? *Splendid! Well done!* As I said then -
you are all Heroes! But...I really, *really* wouldn't advise
anyone to deliberately confront or to approach or even
physically attack these beings and creatures, they have the
capacities to, to, let's say, to harm you, on many levels...*what
they are capable of when under direct threat is probably
beyond what you can imagine at the moment...*

"...But, let's not dwell on that! What they did was *'run away to fight another day'*, there were too many other people around - but they haven't gone away for long...Yes Maria...?" He asked her as she attracted his attention. Maria stood up to speak again.

"You are quite right Anders, and I was going to talk to you about it in more detail later, because I've had so many similar reports come in from most of the others recently - which tend to confirm what you're suspecting. We think it's partly due, at the moment, to a question of their numbers - with so many people now awakening every day all over this planet, from their point of view this is a serious epidemic. So the opposition's Watcher ranks are currently getting very stretched, and thin on the ground, particularly amongst the general mass of humanity – but we do know as well that they are addressing that with a massive recruitment drive - which I also need to talk to you and the others about later as well of course. So - they are reacting to the crisis – crisis for them – *by sending teams of Wreckers directly to the areas around our portal sites* – at least to the ones which they've had a recent breakthrough in detecting.

"...So, we think, that they are thinking, there's no need to have quite so many of the Watchers now around the portal sites they detect, because they can be more usefully deployed in the general human mass areas where they only suspect the awakening is starting to happen...You'll remember Anders, as you've just been saying, the sort of strategies and tactics they used during The Inquisition here, when a, a similar awakening erupted...*but that one, they, they managed to, to contain.*"

Maria paused and shuddered, as if she too was personally recalling many heart rendering memories of those terrible times...

Sophie said in a low voice to Jake, *"Now she's doing it as well!"* Jake frowned not sure what she meant.

"She's doin' what Soph'?" He asked her, looking quickly over to Maria.

"No not *doing*! - Saying! - Well, you might think I'm being a bit daft, but sometimes when Anders was talking and now she's doing it as well, about, about people and things from long ago, it's well, it's as if they knew them or were actually there, and now and again they just let it slip in, but that's just me being daft isn't it? Got to be...! *Hasn't it?!*"

"'Ey! - You're the last person I'd ever call even a slightly bit daft Soph'! An' anyways, y'can't be, 'cos I might sometimes be *a big thick Yorkshireman – but I'm not daft! - 'Cos I've noticed that as well!* But I didn't want to say 'owt, in case y'thought that, that - *I was bein' a bit daft!*"

Sophie tittered and said, "So...as two definitely *non-daft people* then, we both agree, both think, that they might be dropping some sort of...*hints...*?!"

"Aye, I reckon I do! *'Cos what I've 'eard and seen so far tonight has well changed what I'd've said is possible and what ain't possible before...!*"

By now Maria had composed herself and was talking again.

"Oh, please do excuse me everybody, *it's just that sometimes...*So...because they know that there will definitely be larger concentrations of powerfully awakened humans, and especially of the psychically developing humans around the portal areas, who are a greater immediate threat to them, they want to target them first. Especially in the days after your, Anders, and the others', first presentations, as rapidly and powerfully awakening people will naturally be drawn to return, to learn more, and so develop faster by being offered and accepting our guidance...just like here, tonight...

"So our thinking is that their strategy now is to send in Wreckers straight away, to attempt to, as you have described to everyone, to, at the very least, *'dampen down'* those who are awakening and are powerfully psychically *re-developing* as they return...

"...To put it crudely, without any of you having some form of psychic protection, for the opposition it would be like shooting fish in a barrel...or to them it's like a forest fire – where they don't need to have lots of Watchers as an early alarm system, because they already know the fire has started and might be taking hold! And which, most likely, if it's unchecked, will spread rapidly out of control from that area and move into others. So they need to have their actual fire fighters – the Wreckers, already on site and ready to deal with the outbreaks immediately..."

"Yes...yes. Thank you Maria, very well put. I must admit that I had a, a general headline communication..." He tapped the side of his head knowingly, "...about this and some other related matters, but I have been so busy today that I didn't have the time to *fully* go into it – but just the outline of the threat awareness analysis prompted me to action some steps against it in the meantime - *which I'll reveal to you all in a minute.* But you have verbalised it all most eloquently for me and for everyone here, so thank you Maria!"

Looking over again to Jake, he said, "Well, I think with all that it was Maria who has just fully answered your question for you! So now you know, or have some idea of who and what they were...*and well done again for bravely confronting and countering them...!*"

Jake was slowly nodding his head and blowing out his cheeks thinking that he'd had a few *'confrontations'* over the years...but tonight was a first! – At least those in the past he'd come up against had just been 'normal blokes' – well, mebbe not so normal, usually they'd just been 'wired-up-wrong-prats' – *but at least they'd been all human!*

Anders then looked at everyone with his benign expression.

"The beauty of Teamwork eh?! And I am certain that all of you will be relieved to have just heard that we too have an immediate counter strategy in place to the developments that Maria has explained!"

He paused momentarily, nodding to all as they visibly and audibly expressed their relief.

"But to be more precise - *it is you, all of you, who already have it!* But it has been hidden from you. So what we, or rather, friends of ours, can do tonight, a little later, is guide you to start to re-discover and re-use the strategy, the technique, for yourselves...you just need to be reminded of it, because, well - *because you always could!*...So when I say *'we'* have a counter strategy, I don't mean that *'we'* as outside entities are going to come charging over the hill like the Cavalry coming to the rescue in a cowboy film, *and do it all for you,* we can't do that...that would not be allowed...*but you can! - By becoming your own Cavalry!"*

There was an expected uncertain response from everyone to this. From all, that is, apart from Jake who whispered in dead pan humorous enthusiasm to Sophie, *"Oh Magic! – I always fancied bein' a cowboy! – I've even gotta cowboy hat as well!"*

"Whaat!" She whispered, quickly leaning away and looking back at him in apparent shock...

"...You, you fancy...a cowboy?!"

"Ey?! Er, No! Tut! I said...*I fancy bein'....*Huh! Anyway stop interruptin'!...*I'm listenin'!"* He said in mock admonishment, turning his head away pompously, nose in the air, and peeked down at her out of the corner of his eye, trying not to grin. Sophie snuggled herself back under his arm, her shoulders shaking with barely restrained mirth but managing to whisper, *"...Bet you look good in a cowboy hat..!"*

Anders said, "Let me explain – my goodness! *I do seem to*

have said that a lot tonight! I really hope you aren't all getting fed up with me saying that?!" He said with gentlemanly charm, and smiled at the eager and positive replies from everyone for him to continue.

"Thank you all, *thank you!* - You're all very patient and tolerant to an old man!"

Mmm, Sophie thought, *just how old…?!*

"Okay then, well...Before I arrived here this evening, I was meeting with, with friends, who had offered to help with implementing one of your counter strategies, which is the main reason I was slightly delayed getting here, and I believe that some of you may have already briefly met some of those friends of ours before you arrived here?! - Gypsy Magda Leah Rose for one? – She and all her sisters are here at the Fair, there are seven sisters all together!"

"*- We've met her!*" Sophie said out loud, "She spoke to me and Jake, she came out of her caravan, as if she knew we were coming, and, and she said things that, that now, well, make sense, *I think,* and she wanted to, well, she wanted us to see her later...*said she could help...?"*

"Aye! That's right! - An' she knew both our names as well! - *An' we've never seen 'er before!"* Jake also said out loud.

Most of the others then also joined in as well, saying more or less the same things, but not all of them had seen or spoken with the same Gypsy lady that Sophie and Jake had, most said that they had been approached quite early on, or just when they had arrived at the Fair, some contacts had even been in the car park field before they went in to the Fair, by traditionally dressed Gypsy looking ladies and girls who had just walked straight upto them...

Anders smiled. *"Splendid! It sounds like Magda and her good sisters have all been very busy!* - More of that Great Teamwork! And they are clearly no longer complete strangers to most of you then!"

Still smiling he asked them, "Did any of you get a, a feeling of sudden warmth and light all around you, and within you just for a second or two - before you parted company from the good ladies...?" For a few moments, as everyone cast their minds back, the room went quiet, then a hubbub of voices erupted agreeing that they had.

Nodding his head, and still smiling Anders said, "Well, those feelings were due to, what you might more easily understand at the moment, by calling them parts of a Spell, a Spell of Protection they cast around you. It temporarily shielded and protected you, for a while, with the intention of it being, hopefully, to give you enough time to find your own way here...

"When those of you who later felt the headaches coming on, the spell had obviously worn off, or was wearing off, and the Wreckers following you had started to break through it and connect to you...but those of you who came more or less straight here – or straight to where the marquee was last night, and asked Eddie or Bert on the merry-go-round where it had gone, you would have been under its protection long enough to repel any attempts to negatively connect to you. But if you took much longer to arrive, as I said, it would have been

160

starting to wear off, or even have gone completely.."

The girl sat with her boyfriend who had spoken out previously, then hesitantly voiced the question that everyone else was thinking, "So...what happens...now? *How do we...do...what you were saying...to protect us...ourselves...?*"

"Good question!" Anders replied, "basically, you will all leave here soon – not all at the same time, but with just a couple of minutes or so between you, through the door, and, er, re-emerge in, in Magda's caravan, which is quite small – on the outside...but much bigger and quite different on the inside as you'll see...!

"...I think you will all be quite intrigued when you see it...! The Sisters will be there and ready for you all by then and they will explain and show each of you how to enable a psychic protection around you, as and when you need one. It will take some practice – so I'm afraid there's a bit more Homework for you!

"And they will also explain how you can develop your

ability, your visual acuity to see the auras of all other living entities, so that in future you will be able to not only recognise just the auras of the Watchers and the Wreckers, even if they are hiding in a crowd. Actually they are quite easily spotted because their auras are tainted, muddy and dark, like shadowy overlays…

"There are many other - human looking beings in their physical form, that move around *on* your planet, but they have subtly different auras to 'normal' humans. Some of those beings you might see are non-terrestrial, and some are of this planet… And there are some human, animal and bird like entities, that have no auras…they will look, on their outside, to be perfectly 'real', but they are bio-constructs, clones sometimes, a lot of them are controlled by artificial intelligence…and other similar, exotic technologies…! Anyway, at another time, as and when you have seen all of this, and them, for yourselves, I, or another of us, will gladly explain further…"

Sophie felt a sudden flush of excitement, the same sort of feeling that she used to have just before going on a school trip to somewhere that she'd been looking forward to going to for ages – and the day had finally arrived at last! The good feeling outweighed most of the other, disturbing feelings, caused by the rather ominous information that Anders and Maria had both revealed.

In fact, she clearly remembered just then how excited she had been on her first trip to a zoo as a very young child, as she had been constantly amazed at the variety of living creatures she'd seen that day. *Ha!* Sounded like there had been, and still was, a zoo of a very different kind out there and all around her and everyone else all along, and I'm going to be seeing it soon! she thought - by learning how to see auras! *Wow! How cool's that?! Could I really do that?*

Everyone else was talking loudly together. Anders had moved over to speak to Maria, so Sophie sat up and looked at Jake with an impish expression on her face, and speaking in a cheeky little girl-ish voice she said to him,

"*Hey! – I'll show you mine – if you show me yours...?!*" Jake smiled, his eyebrows raised, "*'Ey?* Oh! *Aye!* - Ha! - *Best offer*

I've 'ad all day...!" He laughed quietly with her.

Anders had moved back to the coffee bar counter and he coughed lightly to get everyone's attention again.

"Can I suggest that we have a coffee break now, whilst Maria contacts Magda and sets up your departure, and it'll give me some time to come round, sit down and chat to some of you before you go, does that seem like a good idea to you all?"

Clearly it did, because as well as several voiced agreements to him there was a general shuffling of chairs as people gradually stood up, stretched, and moved over to the coffee bar's long counter to order their drinks.

"One large black coffee wiv a dollop o' cream an' a plate o' choccy biccies all ready f'you Mr. S.!" Announced Alfie all in one quick breath as he placed them on the counter for him, and he then started taking orders, quickly placing cups onto the ancient looking coffee machine, muttering to himself that he'd ,*'have to ask our Eddie to sort the bloomin' thing out and fix it!'* - as the machine seemed to be revelling in zapping his

164

fingers with little jets of scalding steam!

Expressing his thanks to Alfie, Anders retrieved his coffee and plate of biscuits, moving away to let others get to the counter, and he went to a table in the middle of the room where a middle aged lady was sitting on her own waiting for her friend to get their coffees. He asked her if he might join her, then sat down and they started talking.

The jukebox clicked and whirred again as a record was automatically selected and the original 1967 'Jungle Book' song: *'I Wanna Be Like You'* started to play.

" - D'y'fancy another coffee Soph'?" Jake asked her.

"Oooh yes please! Black no sugar! *Could I have some choccy biccies as well please?!"*

"Yes Modom, of course Modom, straight away Modom!" He replied, sounding exactly like Parker from the 60s T.V. series 'Thunderbirds'. He stood up, straightening his back from sitting for so long, then he put his hands on his hips, bowing

165

his legs apart, and in a voice this time sounding exactly like John Wayne's slow western drawl, he said, "Weellll, as ah'm now gonna be a real live cowboy, an' int' Cavalry as well - ah guess ah'd better go crush us up some coffee beans with ma gun butt...*ahhh, goddammit! Ah cain't find mi gun...!*" He patted himself down frantically as if searching for his six shooter...Sophie laughed at his voice impressions and funny antics.

"Jus' go get the coffees Johhhn!" She said in a similar but feminine drawl, and then as he moved away she said to his back, *"An' down't y'forgit ma choccy biccies Johhhn boy!"* He put his arm out with his thumb up in acknowledgement, his back to her as walked away bow legged, making her giggle at him.

Wow! She thought. *What a great bloke He Is!* Just shows you! If you just judged a book by its cover, you'd never've thought that that big, usually quiet and shyish man, mebbe a bit intimidating looking, always unshaven and with long straw coloured hair, wearing an old leather bike jacket with a motorcycle club's back patch on it could be so, well, so nice and so caring and so funny and yet... she remembered how his eyes had narrowed and changed to hard grey flint on the merry-go-round, and before that - when he'd charged without any hesitation at all at those two men, to, to defend her...there was obviously another side to him that was fearless and more than capable...

She smiled even more widely to herself then as she remembered that he'd seemed so nervous though about giving her that first big hug and kiss on top of her head, when he'd picked her up, and then saying to her what he'd eventually said, almost shyly mumbling it at the end – *than he had been going to take on two men all on his own!* Amazing!...And everything they had listened to tonight - at least she had had an introduction to it last night – but he'd just had the whole lot dropped on him in one go with *no idea before it* that it was going to be anything like this! But he'd taken it all on board, processed it and seemed okay with it. *Wow!*

As her nice thoughts continued along in that vein she looked around her and noticed Maria. She was sitting completely still with her head slightly bowed, her eyes closed and the extended forefinger of each hand touching each side of her head. She looked as if she was in a deep meditative trance Sophie thought, or...*oh my God!* Anders had said Maria was going to contact Magda and her sisters – and it looks like it wasn't going to be contact by using her mobile! - There's no signal in here anyway! So - she's – she's obviously doing it with her mind! – Somehow she's doing it...what – telepathically?! *Oh wow! Is she?* Can she really...?! *Is that poss...?!*

"Hi again!" She then heard a girl's voice say, interrupting her thoughts. *"I'm Melanie – Mel..!"*

Sophie looked up and saw the girl she had spoken briefly with earlier – the girl who had been sat with her boyfriend, who'd said they'd seen...*them*...as well.

"Oh Hi! I'm Sophie! *Sorry!* – I was just looking at Maria – *have you seen...?"*

"Yeah, Dave – he's my boyfriend, saw her start doing it, he's gone now for some coffees, he said she must be, that they all probably, must be, well, sort of well, *telepathic...! How weird is all this...?!"*

"*I Know!* Hey – grab some chairs, come and join us, Jake's getting coffee as well – and choccy biccies!"

"Oh yeah, thanks, great! You don't mind?" Mel said, then pulled two chairs over closer to the table, and sat herself down, sighing loudly.

"I could *so* use a de-stressing chocolate boost as well! *Definitely a good idea right now!* But I forgot to ask Dave to get me some, I was too gob-smacked with what that Maria was doing...*and with everything else as well!*" She looked over to the busy and noisy crowd at the counter, "Ah well! *Too late now!*"

"Hey – no probs - you can share ours! – I'll bet you anything Jake brings back far too many biccies, cakes and anything else that's on offer! - First time we went out, on his bike, we stopped at a village cafe on the way back and he ate more sticky chocolate cake than I do in a month! *Couldn't believe it!*" She laughed, Mel joining in with her.

"It's not fair is it! So does Dave! - *If I had a tenth of what he eats I'd put two stones on!"*

They laughed together again, the ice broken, both of them sensing that they liked each other, and were just happy to girl talk and laugh about some lighter, more normal things...for a while, and they continued chatting, and swapping brief details about themselves.

Jake soon arrived back at the table, he had brought two trays, one with two full coffee cups on saucers with a milk jug and sugar cubes in a bowl, and, just as Sophie had predicted, the other tray was full of chocolate biscuits and several large wedges of chocolate cake and chocolaty sticky buns piled up on it! He nodded in a friendly manner to the girl with blonde, spiky, short pixie style hair sat talking with Sophie, and said, *"I was feelin' a bit peckish like!* All that listenin's been 'ard work! *Tired me out!"*

"Oh Wow Jake! - Didn't anyone else want any?! Sophie laughed.

"'Ey? Oh! Oh yeah – *oh there's loads! Best selection*

o'cakes at a cafe I've seen for a long time! Ha! Was just goin' to say we ought t'come 'ere more often! But..."

"Jake – this is Melanie – Mel, she and Dave, her boyfriend, y'know - we spoke earlier - they saw *them* as well..."

"Oh yeah! Hi Mel, I'm Jake!" He put the trays down onto the table and held out his big hand to shake hers, as he sat down next to Sophie.

"Hi Jake. Nice to meet you! – Nice to meet you both!"

"Yeah, nice to meet you too, er, d'y'both want some cake? Think now I might've actually 'ad eyes bigger than me stomach when I got all these…!"

Mel giggled and said, "Oh are you sure? You don't mind? Well yes then, *please!* I forgot to ask Dave to get me some!"

She then looked round to see where he was, and smiled as she saw him move away from the counter and start walking over towards them.

"Here he is!" Her boyfriend, Dave, arrived carrying just one tray.

He smiled at Mel and said 'hellos' to the pretty girl with long black hair and to the big chap sat next to her with a pile of cakes and buns on a tray in front of of him, who he had just seen when he was on his way over to them, hold out his tray for Mel to take a large slice of chocolate cake off it!

"Ah! I got the coffees – and some surprise chocolate biscuits as well for you Mel! - But I didn't know you were going to raid someone else's cake supplies first though!" He laughed.

"Nah that's alright mate! I offered, think I got a bit carried away wi' all this lot!" Jake replied smiling through a mouth full of cake. "Hi, I'm Jake an' this is Sophie, 'ow y'doin? Grab a seat – 'elp y'self to some cake – before Soph' eats it all!"

"Ooooh! – 'Scuse me!! *Cheek!"* Sophie spluttered with mock indignation, munching on a biscuit.

Grinning, Jake wiped his hand on a napkin and stretched his long arm out over the table to shake hands with Dave, who put his tray down onto the table, shaking Jake's hand then Sophie's, whilst introducing himself. He then sat down next to Mel, shuffling his chair closer up to hers, and rubbed his shoulder onto hers affectionately.

"Well, Hello then to you both! Er, I think I'm doing alright, so far! Even after all this! *You still ok luv?*" He asked Mel, giving her a quick one armed hug again.

"Yes thanks, much better now – aaah thanks for getting me some chocolate biscuits as well!"

"*I thought you might like some!* I'm good for now with just the coffee though," he said, politely refusing Jake's offer of cake.

Sophie asked, "So, what do you make of all this Dave? - Mel's told me you were both here – well, at the marquee last night, and so was I but I didn't see you two, and Jake's only come, first time, tonight!"

"Phewwww!" He said exhaling loudly, "I think it's going to take me a while for it all to sink in, but I'm on board with what that Anders, and Maria are saying, makes sense of a lot of things, especially as we – and you – actually saw...saw what we all did...Not saying I need to 'see it to believe it' – but it, sort of brings it all home to you, without any doubt!"

"Same 'ere mate!" Jake said. "I 'ad no idea, well, not really, about any of it. But I knew right away that summat funny was goin' on at the Fair – an' anyways I've always thought summat weren't tickin' over an' runnin' as proper as it should be, like, in the World around us tho'..."

"Yeesss... I like that image – you mean, like a, like an engine, that should be revving away smoothly, firing on all cylinders, loads of power when you want it, burning the fuel nice and clean – but instead it's spluttering, shaking, rough running and way below power!"

"Yeah – that's it! – Bit like that Alfie's ol'coffee machine over there! *Good coffee tho'!"* Jake replied, raising his cup. The other three laughed, the two girls pleased to see that their men

174

were obviously going to get on as well with each other. Putting his now empty cup down Jake said, "but don't remind me about bloomin' engines not runnin' right – 'ad enough o'that all day today an' for past few days, wi' a bike engine I've stripped, rebuilt, and now 'avin' to part strip again, sometimes they just defy all..." He shook his head, and stuffed another huge wedge of chocolate cake in his mouth.

"Is that what you do, fix bikes?" Mel asked him. Jake nodded to her, his mouth full of cake.

"Well, you do a bit more than that Jake." Sophie said to him – *"You design and build some amazing custom bikes..."*

"Oh Wow!" Dave interrupted her - "So is that, that Triumph chop I saw in the car park yours then Jake?"

Jake nodded, quickly finishing his mouthful of cake, before replying enthusiastically, *"Aye!* It's basically a stripped Daytona, bored out to fourteen 'undred c.c., forks raked, frame re-jigged to a classic chop profile, but wi' uprated rear springer suspension, spray job, and..."

"*Uh Oh Mel!* – Boys' bike talk coming up!" Sophie giggled.

"*'Ey!   'S about time somebody talked about summat important an' interestin' t'night!!*" He said deadpan, but his eyes gave away his amusement at teasing her, as he continued feeding himself more cake.

"That's brilliant." Dave said after laughing at what he'd said, "That – but I meant the bike as well! I look at bikes like that one, and think that, well they're like, well, like superb functional iconic sculptures, that you don't just look at but you directly engage with, use and experience for, for all sorts of positive, fun, and exciting reasons..."

Jake stopped chewing. Looking wide eyed at Dave. He quickly swallowed and slowly said, "*Now that's brilliant!* I'll 'ave to write that down! I've bin strugglin' with what words to put on't front page o' me new website that me mate Karl The Computer Wizard's doin' for me..."

Sophie jumped in excitedly, "- And it's brilliant as well - because it's one of those coincidences – *that aren't really coincidences...!* You've created an answer! So recognise it! *Embrace it!*" She said with dramatic humour, waving her arms in a gesture of embrace – and the half eaten chocolate biscuit she was holding flew out of her hand arcing across the room to hit the far wall.

"Ooops! *Look out! Sorry! Low flying biscuits!*"

" *'Ey!* - If I knew y'were just goin' to throw 'em away - *I'd've eaten 'em!*" Jake chuckled.

Laughter from all of them caused others at the nearby tables to look over, smiling at them.

Sophie quickly picked another biscuit off the tray and said to him,"- but you haven't said anything about Karl The Computer Wizard doing a website for you..?!"

"*Well...*" He started to say, then looked mischievously at Dave and Mel, "*Well, I rarely get chance to get a word in like...*"

Sophie's mouth formed an exaggerated 'O', her eyes wide as she gave out a loud *"Humph!"* And she then copied the way he had earlier pompously turned his head away from her, nose in the air. But she quickly looked back at him and then leant against him in a fit of giggles. Jake put his arm round her, and asked Dave, "So, what do you do mate?"

"Well, I paint and sculpt, I'm an artist, just got some of my work on show in a friend's gallery on Bland's Cliff in the old part of town near the beach, and I'm just waiting as well to see if I've got a post to do some part-time lecturing at the Art College next term - *got to pay the bills somehow, until my art works do – if ever!"* He replied.

Sophie said, "And Mel told me she designs and makes jewellery, and works part-time at a printers doing design layouts, so it's just me with the boring old office job - at the estate agents!"

"'Ey don't knock it!" Jake said to her with a smile, "...at least y've got a full time job! Most folk I know are all strugglin', some of 'em tell me they go for a job – and get told they're over

qualified for it, then they go for another an' they 'aven't got enough or the right ones!! *Can't win!* That's one reason why I want t'try and be independent, 'ave a go at bein' self-employed, an' be me own boss like, but I'll still do me part-time mechanicing at Ol'Billy's garage in town as and when like, 'cos I enjoy it, an' me, Ol'Billy an' the lads all 'ave a good crack."

"I know...*I didn't really mean it like that, I am grateful for it,*" Sophie said, "...and *most* of the people I work with are really nice and good fun as well, and it is interesting and...challenging, at times."

The conversation went back to their thoughts about the evening so far, and what they thought was going to happen next. It continued along effortlessly, parts of it straying to comment on the 60's music the jukebox kept playing, the photos' on the walls and about the cafe in general. They all agreed that there must be a market for such a retro style place in Scarborough – or anywhere, today...not that this place was retro...as it apparently just was...somehow, the real thing...Jake managed to finish off all the cakes, buns - and the rest of Sophie's biscuits.

Then Sophie noticed Anders making his way over to them, and tapped Jake's leg rapidly under the table to get his attention, nodding towards Anders.

"*Hello everyone!* How are you all? *May I...?*" Ander's question was interrupted by the tinking sound of a spoon tapping a cup again and they all looked over to where Maria had just stood up.

"Ah! *You're saved by the bell!*" Anders said with a smile to the two young couples.

"Sorry to interrupt everyone," Maria said, "But it's all ready for you now, everything's set up to, to move from here. You do just the same as you did when you came in here earlier, you go through the door, but then up the stairs, and through another door into Magda's...'caravan'. So...and only when you're ready to – perhaps those nearest the door would like to go first...?"

"*That sounds like us then folks!*" Jake said, slapping his hands down onto the table, causing all the cups to rattle on their saucers. He smiled reassuringly to Sophie, Mel and then

Dave, who all suddenly looked a little bit apprehensive.

Anders, noting their apprehension, and then looking around at the others in the Cafe, said loudly, "there is absolutely nothing at all to worry about everyone. I know it must all seem *very strange* to you but I will actually go back and forth with you as well, I'll accompany each of you, or each group, but I just want to say cheerio for now to Alfie...I might be a little busy later so may not get the chance to do so then." He turned to the two young couples and said, "and then we'll all just nip out together – is that okay with you all?"

"Aye mate! No problem. But I'd like to say cheers to Alfie with you as well if that's alright? – *An' I 'aven't paid 'im for all the coffees and cakes yet!*" Jake said.

"*Of course!* Absolutely fine ol' chap! He'll appreciate that! – But don't any of you worry about paying him – he kindly said to me that it's all on the house tonight – partly, and only partly, because the, the currency he uses here is still, well, it's still pre-decimal..'real money' I think he said it was...!" Jake was once again somewhat stunned on hearing this, and so were the other three at the table. But Jake found his voice after a moment or two to say a bit sheepishly, *"Oh Blimey!* I feel right guilty now! *I 'ad loads of 'is cake!* An' coffees! But I wouldn't 'a...."

"- Don't worry about it!" Anders chuckled – "He will be delighted that you enjoyed them! And I know his wife will be too! – She does all the baking for the cafe, but she couldn't be here tonight."

Having said that he then started to move away unhurriedly over to the counter, and Jake, Sophie, Mel and Dave all stood up together to follow him, to say their goodbyes as well, and to give their thank yous to the kind and comical Alfie. The juke box was now playing 'It Might As Well Rain Until September', by Carole King.

After much hand shaking and expressions of their gratitude and thanks to Alfie, the four of them with Anders in front, then walked back towards the photo covered door. As they passed the others at their tables the two girls gave small waves and said quiet *'see you soons'* to them. The two girls were putting on brave faces despite feeling quite nervous now. Jake and

Dave strolled nonchalantly along trying to appear relaxed and at ease so as not to make the girls anymore nervous than they were, Jake giving the positive thumbs up gesture to everyone as they passed.

"Oh, I feel really sad to leave here now! What a nice man Alfie is, and what a great place this is – *do you think we'll ever see it again..?"* Sophie blurted out almost tearfully as they got to the photo' covered wall where the door had reappeared.

On hearing her say this Anders paused, turning back towards her, great compassion in his eyes, and he said reassuringly to her, "Oh...Please don't be sad! I've absolutely no doubt at all that you'll all be back in The Trocadero many, many times in the future – *or in the past!"* A warm, enigmatic smile on his face.

"There see!" Jake said, putting his arm round her and squeezing her shoulders, comforting her.

" - An' I'm gonna miss 'is chocolate cakes until then an'all!"

She looked up in to his face and smiled, putting her arm

around his waist, leaning her head onto him, his humour and Ander's words dispelling her feelings of sadness at leaving.

"Back in a minute!" Anders then said loudly to everyone else in the room, as he opened the door and went through it. He stood on the bottom step as Jake, then Sophie, then Mel and Dave gathered round, the door closing silently this time behind them. "Everyone in?!" Well done! Good Oh! - *Onwards and upwards then! Let's go shall we!*" Anders said light-heartedly.

CHAPTER 4:

The 'Gypsy Caravan'

J ust as they started to climb back up the stairs Jake said to
Anders, "that Eddie must've oiled the door's hinges – they
made a right creakin' noise when he opened it for us before..."

"Ah, well spotted!" Anders replied. *"Not 'oiled' exactly –*
when portal doors make that noise it's an audible warning, like
an alarm, that it's been...sensed, I suppose is the best way to
describe it...by those whom we certainly don't want it to be! If
it's *actual location* had been discovered – it would not have
opened, so Eddie will have closed down that portal as soon as
he got back, that's why he would've dashed off and no one else
came through it after you two did, I came in through this one, it
may look like the same steps and tunnel but it's a completely
different portal..."

It seemed quite dark at first in the earthen tunnel after the bright lights in the cafe, but this time yellow lights in the steps safely lit the way as Anders lead them upwards.

Well at least there aren't as many steps going up this one as there had been in the other one when we came down, Sophie thought, seeing that Anders was already opening another door, and stepping through it.

Soft, warm lighting spilled out from where he was now standing, just inside whatever lay beyond, casting him partly in shadow, as he courteously held the door open for them. Jake ducked down a little to pass through first, Sophie, clinging tightly to his hand, was a step behind him and passed through the doorway and into...

"Ohhhh...Wowww!" Was all she could manage to gasp in complete astonishment, and she looked up quickly to Jake, whose eyes and mouth were open wide in amazement too as he looked into the room beyond. Then she looked quickly over to Mel and Dave - whose reactions on entering were pretty much the same...

"I did say you might find it...*somewhat intriguing!*" Anders chuckled. "It is certainly quite a surprise as well - the first time you see this lovely room!"

"Hello...Again...My...Dears."

The gentle, kindly voice of Gypsy Magda Leah Rose said to them in a warm and friendly greeting as she seemed to glide towards them to stand in front of them all. *How does she do that?* – Sophie thought. *And - and she looks a lot younger now!* about my Mum's age, not my Granny's - like she did before! - *Just How did she do that?!*

"Welcome! Sophie and Jake, Melanie and David! To my...and my Sisters'...'caravan'...!"

"Do excuse me - I'll be right back with more of our guests in just a minute Magda!" Anders said quietly and quickly to her, she smiled and nodded to him, then he politely squeezed past the two young couples, almost unnoticed by them, as they were staring at everything at once, just trying to take it all in, overcome by the sheer size of the immense and luxurious room, and by the six other girls and ladies who were all quietly standing in a line, facing them, about a normal room's length away.

Sophie was thinking that you could get about fifty normal rooms at least in here! And how high is that ceiling!? The four of them weren't even fully aware that Anders had already left, going quickly back down the steps after closing the door silently behind him.

"Please do come in! Melanie and David I am so pleased to meet you both! My name is Magda Leah Rose, but please just call me Magda, and may I introduce you all to my Sisters?"

Magda's hands had been steepled in front of her, her long red painted finger nails just under her chin, and she now turned slightly to the side and swept her arm over towards her six Sisters.

Her Sisters were all quite similar in looks, they all had the same very long reddish auburn hair, but in a variety of sophisticatedly coiffured styles, and they all had the same intensely sparkling emerald green eyes. They were all dressed in long flowing different pastel coloured satiny dresses, Magda was wearing a yellow one, they looked a bit like saris Sophie thought. And then she asked herself again– *how do they do that?!* – As they all seemed to just glide slowly over the creamy beige marble flooring towards them, their long dresses shimmering as they moved.

Closer up now she could see that they were all younger looking than Magda, her youngest Sister is about my age she thought. The Sisters had all had their hands in front of them in the same steepled gesture that Magda had before, but they lowered them to their sides and slightly bowed their heads in greeting, as they stopped a few paces away in front of the two young couples. The Sisters all said *'Hello And We Welcome You'* at the same time, their voices combining in a delightfully sing-songing feminine chorus.

The two young couples, awed and mesmerised by it all, bowed their heads slightly as well, copying the way the Sisters had, and said their 'Hellos' to them in return.

Magda smiled and said, "Now – *Don't worry!* - I'm not going to overwhelm you by immediately giving you a long list of all my Sisters names - all at once! – You can introduce yourselves properly and talk – if not with all of them later on this evening there will be many other occasions, as time goes by...So...because we met earlier..." She looked directly at Sophie and Jake, "...and you have come now with your new friends, shall we five all go together and find somewhere to sit down? And then I can talk and explain...various things for you..."

Magda turned and started to move away from them so they could follow her into the immense room. Oh! She's actually walking now – not gliding! Sophie thought – as Magda lead them towards the first in a long row of matching, cloister like, wide marbled archways all along one side of the vast room. Beyond the archway she was leading them to, they saw that it lead into an alcoved area the size of a normal house's lounge.

As they neared the alcove, inside it they could see there were two extra long Chesterfield sofas covered in a reddish brown silky fabric, two matching high backed winged chairs and several low, oriental looking, round, black and gold lacquered tables placed unobtrusively but conveniently near to the seating.

Magda looked back over her shoulder to them saying, "...some of our other guests who will be arriving soon - the people you saw and met in 'The Trocadero', have already, even though just briefly, met some of my Sisters, earlier this evening, at the Fair, so we thought it would be nice for each guest to see a familiar face again to personally greet them and talk with them now! - Ah! I see that Anders has already come back with more guests!"

The two couples glanced behind them and saw that Anders had indeed already returned, this time with the two middle aged ladies whose table he had been sat at earlier, before he had come over to theirs.

As they continued walking behind Magda, Jake said to none of them in particular, "Well... I 'ave to say, I've been in a lot o'caravans, on fam'ly 'olidays an' that as a kid, an' I've even lived in one once on a farm for a year or so– but I'd no idea that

191

Romany caravans were like this...*bigger ont' inside than ont' outside!*" As he kept swivelling his head around to take it all in. *"It's like a, a room in a palace or a stately 'ome!"*

Sophie said, "I know...that's right...it's just like one! I went to Chatsworth House in Derbyshire once – and it's just like some of the amazing rooms in there – but much bigger! It's just too incredible! – *Well...you did say 'it looked a classic' when you first saw it!"* *Can tonight get any weirder?!* She then thought to herself.

"Aye I did! – And that were just on't outside!" He chuckled. "What about you Dave, Mel – you ever...?"

Mel said, *"I've never even been inside a caravan before! -* I didn't realise I was missing out on so much! She chuckled. *"Not that I think for a moment that this a caravan! -* You have though haven't you Dave?"

"Yes – my parents still have a static, holiday one, on a site at Filey, it's, it's, er, *just a little bit different to this though...!"*

Magda quietly laughed as she listened to them. As they all approached the seating area, she invited them with a sweeping arm gesture to choose where they wanted to sit. Jake and Sophie sat closely together on one of the oversized sofas, Jake carefully putting the helmet bag with the glass vase in it between his feet. Mel and Dave sat in the other one facing them, and then Magda moved over to sit in one of the matching high backed chairs placed between and at the far end of the sofas at a right angle to face them all.

When they had all settled she said, with laughter still in her voice, "I am so pleased you all like it! All of us have added our own individual touches to it over the years, so it is unique in its own décor, but there are many more, all basically similar to it that others have…And they are all quite delightfully different!"

"Well, it's certainly a lot more than – *'intriguing'* and *'quite surprising'*…like Ander's understatement!" Dave said, "and it's not an illusion – because we're sat in it! So, I've got to ask – where is it? - Where are we? Aaand how? - *How is all of this possible?"*

Magda lowered her head slightly in thought, then she looked up at Dave, and then looked around at each of their expectant faces before replying.

"Well...we are not *in* the caravan of course, technically speaking that is in a different part of the, the third dimension, where it has a portal door to access this room. Later, when you leave here, you will go through that portal door which is next to the one you all just came into here through. Then you will walk along a short corridor and emerge into the caravan..

"This room you are in exists...let me just say for now...in a different part or layer of the same third dimension. Each dimension actually has many layers to it, there isn't a hard and well defined boundary where one dimensional layer finishes and the next one starts...like countries are drawn on a map with definite borders around them..."

She saw the confusion on their faces and smiled, "...for example - let's look at a rainbow so you can all actually see what I mean..."

Magda then held her arms about a yard apart, just below shoulder height, her palms facing upwards, closed her eyes for a second, and then as she opened them - a large bright rainbow appeared arcing from one hand to the other...!

"Now...at first glance - it looks as if there is a definite ending of one colour and the starting of another doesn't it...?"

She looked up, and saw that none of the four young people sitting in front of her were capable of anything approaching coherent speech right at that moment, as they were all just staring wide eyed at the glowing rainbow that had suddenly appeared, as if by magic, between her hands.

"Oh - this rainbow is *a thought form*, you will soon learn that *thoughts are actually 'things'* - but we'll go into all of that another time – or, even, perhaps just a little later on tonight...so...for now, just watch closely..."

She slowly moved her hands together, and like rapidly zooming in to an on-screen digital photo after a moment all that was visible of the rainbow was a red band fading into the

195

next orange band. Then she moved her hands even closer together, zooming in further until there was no distinctly red or orange colour but a blending, of an area showing only the blurring of the many shades from pure red to pure orange.

"There! Now can you all see the many subtle shades?! With no distinct boundaries! Does that help to show you what I mean?"

Mel managed to say: *"Wow!* Yes it does! But I never...never really thought of it, never really even thought to think to look at it like that before...to describe...it...dimensions...and things..."

Sophie looked at Jake and then over to Dave, they were both leaning forwards, very still, and so deeply in thought, staring at where the full rainbow had been, that she thought she could almost hear the cogs turning and whirring in their minds!

Magda continued, "So, between the dimensions there are all of these...let us call them *hinterlands*...which from a distance..." She moved her hands widely apart again, the full rainbow reappearing as distinct and separate colours, "...are hinterlands that are normally just about impossible to see...but *within* the dimensions they are large enough for whole, well - *cities and more - to exist in...at the same time...and in more or less the same place!*"

Magda closed her eyes for a second, moved her hands together in a soundless clap, and the rainbow disappeared. She opened her shining emerald green eyes looking at each of them in turn, then asked them all again, "I hope that helps you to understand...*even just a little... for now?*"

Jake cleared his throat and said, "Aye, aye it does...*I think!...*" He shuffled to sit fully back into the comfy sofa, before continuing, "...an' to me, to me at any rate, y'know I've always 'ad a feelin', said so in in the cafe before, but never could quite put me finger on it, but it's getting' so dead obvious to me now, that...well, that basically everythin' just i'n't what it seems, or is said to be..., y'gotta look at it all a lot closer, like y'just did...seems there really is a load more goin' on in this world than at first seems...to...be seemin' to be goin' on...!?"

He shrugged in frustration, saying, "...Wish I'd listened more now to them borin' English classes when I were at school - 'stead o' messin' abaht!   Then I'd prob'ly be better able to explain proper, to er, explain more...*of exactly what I mean...!*"

Magda smiled at him. "Well Jake I think you, and all of you, are doing wonderfully!   Considering the newness and the strangeness of everything – *and all at once* - for you all so far tonight...!

"But you mentioned your schooling...well, your schools and your educational institutions, which you have all gone through, and which I call *'programming warehouses of the young'*, amongst other, even less pleasant descriptions, hardly encourage the young to learn about how they can fully utilise and engage with their right brain.   Because if they did they would learn, from a very young age, how to think at much higher levels.   And to learn about how to use all of their potential creativity, expansively and truly originally...and then also think and critically question the things they are told to just accept as fact, and then lucidly express those higher thoughts and insights...when they discover - for themselves - that not everything they are being told is factual at all...

"...So why is that?...Why don't they encourage and nurture those ways of thinking?...Well, it is because at first they want to limit your perception, which leads you by the hand on to all of your beliefs - *and in particular your belief of what is 'possible'* – so it is programmed and manipulated to be narrow, tiny, constrained and locked in – as a default setting - during your very young and most vulnerable, formative years. Locked in to a-left-brain-five-senses-only, materialistic, very limited, and essentially, a very false perception of reality, and therefore of course a very limited sense of what is...*really possible.*

"Because when they achieve all of that it means that you can be more easily controlled, programmed and trained to be merely unquestioning repeaters of the supposed facts of the curriculum, and its latent agenda.

"Oh - with any agenda there are are always *two* components to it – the *'manifest agenda'*, that which on the surface is the 'official' reason given for it, and then there is the *'latent', or hidden agenda,* which is, of course, it's real purpose...For example...Whilst we are on the subject of 'education'...let me quote to you what the journalist, author and scholar, Henry Mencken, who was called 'The Sage Of Baltimore', one of the most influential American writers of the first half of the twentieth century, said about educating the public, he said:

'...The aim of 'education' is not to spread enlightenment at all, it is simply to reduce as many individuals as possible to the same level, to breed a standard citizenry, and to put down dissent and originality...'

"...So...When you take their 'educational' tests and their examinations...they say...*'you must repeat just what we have told you - to pass them - and to succeed'*, and those presenting it, entraining and programming you, have gone through the same process as well, and most of them are just as unaware, just as unquestioning...

"I was talking to a young mother the other day and she was infuriated that her son's class at his school, they are only five year olds, were starting to do a term's project all about Egypt, and those little ones had been told, quite emphatically, by their teacher, that the pyramids were: a) built by the Egyptians, and b) they built them just to put their dead Pharaohs in! When she complained to the school, pointing out many facts that totally negate those 'facts' - which are actually just theories, the Headmaster apparently said to her, 'well, all that maybe...*but we have to teach - only what is on the curriculum given to us...*'

"...They - 'the education system', will say, '*you must take in and believe what we tell you...to pass our exams'...! To qualify...! To get a job! To succeed..! Because then you'll be streets ahead of those who don't...!*' My reply to all of that is: *Yes! Of course you will be streets ahead!*" She then sighed and said – "*But On The Road to Nowhere...*"

She sighed again, "Compared to the paths, streets or roads that you could be on in your true reality, *it is* 'The Road To Nowhere' – well – not exactly 'nowhere' – but that destination they've set out for you is a place far, far away from where you should be being guided and helped towards...to being aware of what you truly are and are truly capable of doing..."

"Yeess..." Dave said quietly, "when I went off that road, to do my own thing, just about everyone – my parents, colleagues and even lots of my friends were all dead set against me doing it, but some did say that they *would like to as well, but, but they just couldn't'*...and they had all sorts of, really convincing – to them anyway, reasons why they just couldn't.

"I actually did a painting, a few months ago, about it. I painted a scene of long lines of people, all sorts of people, young and old, they were like all the refugees we see on the television. In my painting they are all carrying all sorts of baggage, marching along on a smooth black road going towards a dark tunnel in the distance – but a few of the people have just thrown all their baggage away, turned off the road, climbed over the barriers – like those in the middle of a motorway but higher – and they're running away over a rocky landscape towards some mountains where the sun is rising – and all the long lines of the other people are waving their arms and look like they're shouting for them to come back...It was sort of how I felt at the time...I suppose! Actually, earlier Anders told us about 'Plato's Cave' – I hadn't heard of it before – it's sort of the same theme, it rang a bell in me when he did.

"But anyway, we're managing aren't we Mel? In fact – *I wouldn't've met you if I hadn't done it!* 'Course you had just taken the plunge and *broken out* as well hadn't you?! And we just sort of, found each other! Seemed like coincidence at the time – but I, we, know a bit more about what *'coincidences'* are now from what Anders was saying...! - And you had the same sort of reactions from others as well didn't you Mel?"

"Yes, I did, not from everyone, but lots of them were like that. Wasn't easy...but...like you say...we met and we're doing okay, well, sometimes not all that okay-ish money wise, but more important than that we feel a lot freer, and much more in control of our lives, *and we're much happier aren't we...?!*" She reached for Dave's hand and squeezed it tightly, as they smiled affectionately to each other.

"Sorry Magda!" Dave said, "I interrupted you, *I can waffle on a bit sometimes!*"

"Not at all! Well done! Both of you. Very well done, and thank you - that was so lovely to hear. You've both been very brave, and I'd love to see your painting sometime David! What

have you done with it?" Magda asked him.

"Oh...thanks! Yeah of course, I'd be interested to hear your thoughts about it! It's now with some others I've done, they're all in an exhibition – my first one! - at a friend's gallery in town – I'll tell you where it is later if you want?!"

"Yes, please do! I shall definitely go and see your exhibition, my sisters will too! - But perhaps not all at once! We all love paintings and art works! Another time when you visit here I will show you round *our* galleries..." She placed her hands down onto the chair's arms, gathering her thoughts back before continuing.

"So from now on, it seems to me that all of you – are no longer going to be - or you are less likely to be...fooled, shall we say...? I recall the sadly insightful words that the author Mark Twain, whose real name was Samuel Clemens, was reported to have said:

'It is so much easier to fool the people - than it is to convince them that they have been fooled...!'

"And in his autobiography he wrote it similarly:

'how easy it is to make people believe a lie, and how hard it is to undo that again!'

"Another of his many insightful quotes was: *'people who don't read the news are un-informed, but those who do are mis-informed!'*

"...Samuel's - or Mark's - erudite comments do go a long way to sum up some of what I know Anders has already talked to you about, of the difficulties you will face sometimes, when you go against the herd, against the group think. - Have any of you watched a flock of sheep being herded by a shepherd and his dog?"

They hadn't – well they had, 'but only on television, not for real', they said. Only Jake said he had for real – "once when I were out on the bike I was goin' a bit fast round the corner of a country lane an' almost ran into 'undreds o' sheep all beltin' across the lane right in front of me! – Bloomin' things nearly 'ad me off the bike! Slammed the anchors on and skidded to a stop just in time! But two sheep dogs soon got 'em into the next field across the road, it was amazin' to see 'ow quick all them sheep just followed each other, and with just two dogs controlled by a shepherd! The dogs were yappin' at 'em and roundin' up them that tried to wander off!'

Magda, nodding as she listened to him, then said, "Yes it is amazing, but just imagine if at first just one, then two, then a few, then a few more and then more, and more, until eventually all those hundreds of sheep had all managed to overcome their fears of just the shepherd and his two dogs, and they had all just gone where their own free will wanted them to go...Those two dogs and the shepherd controlling them would have been powerless to stop that from happening...You can see the analogy with humans, can't you? - replace the dogs with, with *fear* essentially, fear combined with many other subtle, and not so subtle mechanisms, and you can see how the very few can control the very many..."

"Like sheeple!" Sophie interrupted, "I know that doesn't really sound very nice but, I read it somewhere! Can't remember the name of the book...who wrote it, but he, think it was a 'he' – then said, oh what was it?! – Oh Yes! 'A nation of *sheep will soon be ruled by a government of wolves'*, something like that, I thought that was, well, a bit worrying!"

"Well, it's a good way to put it that Soph', sounds about right!" Jake said to her. "Think I'll 'ave to start readin' more! In fact me mate at the garage said 'e was goin' to get me a book for last Christmas, but 'e didn't 'cos 'e said 'e knew I'd got one....!" He said completely deadpan, it took a second for everyone to cotton on to what he'd just said, and then they all laughed.

Magda said to him through her laughter, "Your gift of humour is a truly wonderful thing Jake...despite everything you've experienced this evening, which obviously has to be very unsettling and unnerving for you, for all of you at first, your gift of humour and its positive uplifting effect when you share it with others is a lovely, and a caring thing to do..."

"Oh! Er, well, *thanks!* But I dunno about all that – I've always tried to 'ave a bit of a laugh, used to get told off all the time for it though at school when I were bored, but it just comes natural like, cheers other folk up an' it always makes me feel better as well like...! - Not that we need cheerin' up in 'ere tho' - *with you* - I mean...*well, y'know what I mean...?!"*

"Of course! - And I'm *so glad* you don't need cheering up in here – *and with me!"* Magda replied, teasing him, and laughed along with the others.

"And you are Jake of course more than welcome – all of you are - when you come back here again to browse through our libraries as well, we have all collected many, many thousands of books over the cent...years...!"

She was going to say *centuries!* Sophie thought, *I know she was...!* She looked discreetly over to Dave and Mel to see if they had noticed, Dave didn't seem to have, but Mel had as she was looking wide eyed back at Sophie. They both broke off their eye contact as Magda started talking again.

"But it is amazing how important and how powerful, humour and laughter really are. It changes your brain chemistry, and empowers, repairs and strengthens your body's immunity system...and it makes your *aura* glow even brighter, like a

Shining One!" She smiled, pausing for a moment, before she said,

"...and it takes a very clever person to act the Fool...!"

She paused again, and said, "I'll come back to that - to your *auras* - later, after I've talked about – I've already mentioned it - the 'I' word – 'Immunity'. But first, just to add to talking about humour...it is something that children do naturally of course, and how delightful it is to hear the laughter of children, they all do it so naturally and spontaneously - even those poor little souls in the direst of circumstances that I have been with...

"But so often, over time it gets gradually repressed, and almost drained away, in so many ways, in the milieu of your world where only the left brain's dominance is encouraged, with it's cold, stern logic and rationality, so be serious! Be sensible! Be alert! – Because your country needs lerts!"

It took a few seconds again for them all, including Jake, to cotton on - and then they responded with more laughter at Magda's words.

CHAPTER 5:

A 'Psychic Diamond'

"Well, I really think that we've all, between us, created such a lovely vortex of positive energy around us, that now would be a good time to move onto how to utilise and connect with your positive light energy for your psychic protection that Anders mentioned to you. It is a crucial ability to be able to put it in place at will, it's like quickly putting on a protective suit of armour against, against those whom would want to penetrate and 'dampen you down'...But it doesn't weigh anything at all or restrict your movements in the slightest - or even go rusty!" She laughed.

"I will first explain, and then describe the techniques of implementation, then you can all try it."

Sophie leaned forwards, ready to hang onto every word she was now about to hear.

"Have any of you heard of 'chakras' before?" Magda asked them.

"Yes, I have!" Mel said. "Aren't they sort of like - *energy centres in your body?"*

Dave said, "I read a book a long time ago when I first started to learn about meditation, it mentioned a bit about them, but I can't remember exactly what it said now..."

Jake looked questioningly at Sophie, they both shook their heads at each other.

Magda continued, "Well - you all have them within you! Everybody does! Within the human body are seven *main* chakras, the word *'chakra'* means *'wheel'* in the ancient language of Sanskrit. Each chakra has an attachment to separate body areas. When adepts at meditation describe in detail the chakra-wheel concept, they explain that these 'wheels' normally spin in a circular movement, which makes a vacuum. As a vacuum, a chakra will then pull in physical and mental energies to the body's part that it is connected to.

211

"There are seven separate, but interlinked, chakras, each one basically has that purpose, but they must all work together to create a harmonious balance of energies in your body. When they are all in line and all in balance, you will experience physical and emotional health and peace...

"The first chakra is at the base of your spine.

"The second is near the lower section of your stomach around your navel.

"The third is in the solar plexus.

"The fourth is the heart chakra and is in the middle of your chest.

"The fifth is the throat chakra.

"The sixth is called 'the third eye chakra' it is in the region of your forehead and it connects to your physical body through your brain's pineal gland and nervous system.

"The seventh chakra is the crown chakra, and its position is in the top section of your head.

"This crown chakra controls and conduits your spirituality. When you have this chakra in balance with all of your other chakras you will receive what feels like a, like a flooding of tremendous widespread shining energy throughout your entire being. You will feel linked to the infinity of the multiverse. The sixth and seventh chakras physically affect your body through the pineal gland along with numerous other areas of your nervous system. The crown chakra is in control of the right side of your brain when you meditate."

Magda sat back, giving them a few moments to absorb all of this information.

"Blimey!" Jake said, *"...Didn't get told any o' this in them Biology classes at school! Cuttin' up a dead frog an' lookin' at plant leaves through a microscope were about it...!"*

"No, you certainly would not have been, sadly that is very true Jake, and I will explain more specifically as to why it is later. Now - does anyone remember the sequence of all the colours you saw earlier in the rainbow?" She asked them.

"Ah! Yes I do!" Dave said, "I remember them by saying: 'Richard Of York Gained Battles In Vain!' He shrugged his shoulders self-deprecatingly, "...helps me remember when I'm painting! The first letter of each word is a colour, so it's: Red,

Orange, Yellow, Green, Blue, Indigo, Violet."

"Excellent! That is a good mnemonic memory aid so you won't forget them!" Magda said.

"Colours are energy frequencies, wavelengths of energy you are exposed to that you can see, or, more accurately I should say, they are wavelengths of energy that you take in through the lenses of your eyes, which then travel along the optic nerves, and are decoded by your brain into recognisable 'things' you can 'see'. Red is the lowest frequency you can see or decode normally, and violet the highest, below and beyond those colour frequencies your 'normal sight' cannot decode – so you do not 'see' them.

"Your emotions, which are, in their essence, just energy frequencies as well - but ones that you feel - and you are constantly transmitting, are connected to your chakras. A colour's frequency does have a big affect on your emotions. In your world colours are used all around you by those who understand all of this. At a basic level you will have all heard expressions like: 'I saw red with anger, or I was green with envy, or, I was having the blues..', well, they *simply* express the currently dominating chakra's emotional energy transmission...My favourite colour is yellow, *because it is the colour of hope and optimism...*"

"Yesss, as a painter I've studied the symbology and use of colours - when and why the great painters deliberately used them knowing they'd cause a certain response, feeling, or even reveal a hidden message they wanted to communicate to the viewer – well at least to the viewer who knew what they were looking at, it is really fascinating the more you go into it." Dave said.

"*It is indeed!* And it is not just the great painters who used and use this knowledge of course – for example restaurants often have reddish walls or similar colour schemes because those colours subconsciously evoke your appetite responses! Again, and if only, all of this was taught openly. Anyway, as I've said, there are seven main chakras, and they relate to the seven colours in sequence in a rainbow...Now, let's imagine a circle of each of the rainbow's colours in place around each of your chakras...

"The red circle is near the base of your spine, the orange circle is around your navel, the yellow circle is over your solar plexus, the green circle is around your heart, the blue circle is around your throat, the indigo circle is around your forehead, and the violet circle is around the crown of your head."

Magda then stood up to demonstrate this by touching each part of her body with both hands where the chakras were and repeating out loud the colours for each one.

"Now if all of you wouldn't mind standing up with me as well we can do it together, and then whilst we are all standing we can move on to the process of summoning and implementing your psychic energy shield."

They all stood up and repeated Magda's words and copied her movements several times.

"Well done! She said, "now, the reason for doing that was just to start to familiarise you with the locations and the colours of your chakras within you, and it will help you to remember them, I hope. I am sure you will all be relieved to know though that you will not have to stand in the middle of the street – or wherever you are - and do that every time you want to start to summon your shield!" She laughed. "What you will do then is stand and use your mind's eye *to imagine, to picture* the chakras and colours."

"That's a relief then!" Said Jake - "If I did all this in't street folk's'd all think I'd finally gone doolally…!"

Magda continued after smiling at his comment, "So…! We will remain standing and move onto the next stage. The formation of an immunity energy shield can take a number of shapes…but first imagine a brilliant cut diamond, then expand this into a complete circle or bubble, the bottom of which is just under your feet but above the ground, and the top of it is just above your head.

"Now, from your violet crown chakra draw energy up from your body passing through the base, red chakra and in turn through each chakra as you draw it up. When you have done that the next step is to create a stream of energy emitting from your crown chakra which will feed and support this energy shield. While you are doing this quietly say this mantra:

'I create this impenetrable shield to block and prevent all negative energies from assailing me.'

"Now, as you look at the shield in your mind's eye recreate all the facets of the diamond so that they all twinkle, sparkle and shine with pure white energy.

"When you first implement the shield it is sometimes not possible under normal circumstances to maintain it for very long. With time and practice you will be able to extend its duration. All pure thoughts can pass through this shield to you so positive thoughts will not be impeded. It is only the lower density, lower vibrational thought, negative energy transmissions that will be blocked out...Well then – over to you! - *Now Do It - for yourselves, in your own time!*"

Magda watched them as they all started to concentrate, their eyes screwed up intently, as they attempted to perform the ritual she'd described. She'd deliberately said - *'Now Do It...'* - rather than *'now try it...'* because she knew there was a world of subliminal command difference between asking someone to 'try' something compared to asking them to 'do' something...confidently asking them to 'Do It' was much more likely to help them succeed at it...

After a few minutes she very quietly asked, "Do you now feel any difference? Or see anything different around you?"

Dave replied first saying, "Yeess, I see! Well, in my mind's eye I can see, sort of see, the chakra colours and the white diamond, around me, like you described..." He opened his eyes, and looked down at himself, "Can't see it now!"

Magda laughed, "Well done! Anyone else 'see'...?" She asked.

Sophie said, her eyes still closed, "I think so, but I don't really know if I've done it...!"

"I'm the same, I think, but...am I doing it...?" Mel said.

Sophie opened her eyes and looked at Jake. She saw he was still trying intensely, and she wanted to ask him, but didn't want to interrupt the obvious effort he was putting into it. But he then opened his eyes wide, letting out a deep breath he'd held, which had caused his face to redden. "Mmm, I dunno! I'm more used to doin' and makin' things with me 'ands – things I can see an' touch! 'Ow about you Soph' – 'ow was it for you?!"

"Well, I tried really hard, but I don't really know!"

Magda softly clapped them all saying, "Okay everyone, well done! You did it! Now just relax, release all that effort and forcing, let it all just go and fade away...take some really deep breaths and we will do it again in a minute – but this time do not try to 'force it'. Because in the physical, third dimensional realm of so called 'matter' you are used to applying force, or lots of effort to make and move things - but you are now working in the non-physical realm of energy, *which is what everything...really is anyway,* a 'spiritual' realm, so no physical type of force is necessary, or effective. Instead the way to be effective in this realm is by *Feeling,* and just *Allowing A Knowing, a Knowing Feeling of Certainty that what you desire and so what you intend to create is really manifesting...*start by eliminating *any doubts* about that, and *Just Believe...*So...once more, in your own time, *Do It Again*, when you are ready..."

This time they all looked much more relaxed as they started to attempt it again.

After a while Magda interrupted them again. "Annnnd – relax!... *That was Much Better!* Please sit back down, and relax." She clapped her hands again, louder this time.

As they relaxed and settled themselves back into the sofas, Magda said to them, *"So much information so soon!* So advanced and *so new to you,* and perhaps it all seems difficult to you now - so please do practise it and research it all further in your own time – and you will realise that it is just the beginning of starting to *understand* all this and many more wonderful things you are all more than capable of...an *understanding* which starts with *Knowing, Believing and then Allowing...*

"Let me now tell you all what *I* saw. The first time you all eventually achieved to create the outline, more or less, of the diamond, and make it glow, before it all quickly faded away - but this second time you were all *so much quicker to manifest them completely,* and they all shone *much brighter,* and are only now starting to fade...It is something that with more practice and more, knowing, believing, and allowing, will become automatic, 'second nature', and will surround you much more quickly, and the longer it will remain in place to protect you."

Sophie said, "So, so you could...*can*...obviously see our...our 'diamonds'...Magda?!"

"Oh Yes! I can. I saw them all quite clearly. Just as I can see your auras, and those of all other living beings. In a moment I will explain how you can start to learn how to do that as well...but first, I think I need to explain a little more about...*'Sight'*...and *'Seeing'.*

"...When you see a 'real' rainbow, for example...let's say you are out walking over the lovely moors near Whitby on a sunny morning, when a shower of rain starts to fall – and a rainbow appears! Well, the existence of that rainbow – its existence to you, depends entirely on the millions of conical photo receptors that you, as humans, have in your eyes, and then on your brain's decoding of those signals from them - s*o you see a rainbow!* Now...for animals without those cones in their eyes, *the rainbow does not exist*...so you are not just looking at the rainbow – you are, each of you, effectively, *creating it for yourselves*...from only the tiny, tiny fraction of the full electro magnetic energy spectrum of visible light that you can, currently, decode and then 'see'...!"

Magda looked around at their confused faces, and was about to suggest she explained it again when Jake said,

"Okay...so...say I'm walking over t' moor, takin' 'Butch', me mate's dog - he's a big Alsatian crossed with a yeti – *the dog that is* - not me mate 'Simmo' - *although he could definitely pass for summat like a bald yeti sometimes...!* - for a good walk say, an' I sees a rainbow, so I calls the dog to cum'ere, then I point up to t'rainbow and I says to 'im: 'Look at that rainbow Butch! Great innit?!' - So Butch 'as a good look up, an' then he looks back at me an' he says, *'Er, look at what Jake? – What's up? What's a rainbow?'* Not that Butch can speak tho' o' course..." he grinned. "Apart from when he wants 'is dinner!

All he can see is sky, clouds and rain, so for 'im, you're sayin' then, the rainbow just don't exist...because...like a computer...he 'asn't got some 'ardware parts in 'is eyes that I 'ave, an' he 'asn't got the software parts in 'is brain I 'ave - so I can see that rainbow because all my extra parts 'ave made me able...to see it...?!"

"Well put Jake!" Magda said. "You have explained it with far more clarity than I did! Does it make sense to you all now as well?"

They all nodded in agreement, and Mel said, "Oh dear! I can see – oh! *There's a pun!* - That I'm going to keep on saying - *'I never thought to think of that before'* - a lot tonight!"

"Me too! Don't worry about it!" Sophie giggled. "I thought I felt parts of my brain having the cobwebs blown away before, when Anders was talking – and there's more and more getting blown away every minute now!!" She laughed.

"- There's nothing like a good 'spring cleaning' is there Sophie!" Magda said as she laughed along with her.

"Now, let's see...Ah! - *I've caught your puns Melanie!* Let us go a little further, David – you said something interesting before, well – you said lots of interesting things before! – But the one I'm referring to is when you said: *'...in my mind's eye...'*, when you were talking about creating your diamond..."

"Oh Yeah! I meant, well, like we all do, and you said it as well! We all say 'in my minds eye' don't we? Because you get a picture in your mind, I do when I get an idea for a painting or a sculpture – and Mel, you do when you're making jewellery – don't you – and Jake, I bet you do when you're designing and making a new bike project? So...what's that? I mean, why is it, and how is it, I, all of us can, see...something...in here...?!" He asked Magda, pointing and tapping his forehead.

"Because you can. Because you, and all humans, *are all creators...*" Magda replied.

"...Try thinking about it like this to start with – everything around you in your world, and I don't mean the sea, the moors and the mountains, the sun, the wind, the rain and so on – that's the natural environment, I mean every 'thing' else – the things -

from the clothes you wear, to the houses you live in, to all the thousands of things you use without a second's thought everyday, all of those *'things'*...well, they once only existed - *as a thought, as a vision, in someone's - 'mind's eye'...!* Now that might seem, at first glance, to be just a simple statement of the obvious!...But really think about it...For any-'thing' to exist, and to actually manifest in this physical third dimension, it had to first appear in someone's *'mind's eye'* as a thought, a vision, before it started to go through a...process...to manifest it into a so called 'physical' form, here...

"...Now, most fortunately, there was, and there is, another factor at work in that process – and that factor is called...*Time.* Time, here in the third dimension, has to 'pass' before that thought, that vision in your mind's eye, can be manifested into your 'reality'...Why is that? - Well, just try and imagine what the world would be like if Time had no influence to delay whatever thought visions you constantly have, from moment to moment - from manifesting immediately! – the result? - *Utter chaos!*"

She threw her hands up in a gesture of theatrical despair and pantomimed being overwhelmed, slumping back into her chair, causing much obvious amusement in her audience.

Sophie then said, "But, when you made the rainbow appear, between your hands, I think you said it was *'a thought form'*, but you've just said that time has to pass before, before a thought, a vision can appear – but that rainbow did just appear – *straight away!?*"

"Ah! Yes, yes it did." Magda smiled. "That was what, sometimes, *not quite accurately though technique wise,* is called...magic, yes, in a way it was magic-al I suppose, but that was merely, although *'merely'* isn't really the correct word at all, because it takes a very long, long 'time' to, to learn and to acquire the skills necessary to manifest certain thought forms like that one to be perceived by others immediately, and at will – which is what I did then.

"True Magic is not dissimilar – you all know the words 'abra cadabra'? Well, basically what they actually mean is: *'I Create As I Speak...'* - but magic will have to be a subject we will talk about on another day, or days, or weeks! – I think your bowls might be close enough to overflowing as it is tonight! And I do want to talk some more with you about seeing, and auras...before..."

"But...but before you do...! You're saying...that *actual magic*...really exists?!" Sophie asked her.

"Oh Yes my dear! Of Course! - *It Most Certainly Does...!*" Magda replied.

Oh My God! Sophie thought. If I'd heard that before tonight, from *anyone*, I'd've, well I think I'd've just *'scuttled away'* too like the man did that Anders − Churchill − said he did, but hearing it from Magda...! *Oh My God! So it's all true! All the stories and all the...*

"Yes, they are − *mostly...*" Magda said to her, and Sophie realised she must've been talking out loud after her first thoughts, and she hadn't been alone in doing that, as the others too were now all suddenly talking and asking questions all at once. Magda was answering the questions they were all pouring out with, when another voice broke in upon them saying, "My Goodness! You *are* all *very* busy in this corner! So I thought some refreshments might be needed!"

The voice belonged to the youngest looking of Magda's sisters, and she was carrying five tall glasses of water on a long, ornate silver tray for them.

"Oh Thank You Ruth!" Magda said, "I think a small break now as well would be a very good idea! Ruth - let me introduce you to everyone." After Magda had introduced her sister to them all, Ruth explained that as she didn't have a group to talk to this evening she was just generally helping out and making sure everyone had refreshments, and she pointed over to an arched entrance to a corridor where the bathrooms were for anyone who wanted them, she then left them, walking away with the empty tray.

I suppose she's walking, Sophie thought, as she watched her go, because it would be quite distracting for everyone to watch her just seem to glide around! The two girls decided to go off together to find the bathroom, leaving Jake, Dave and Magda talking amongst themselves. The two girls hardly drew breath as they walked away, chatting and sharing their thoughts with each other. They met and talked as well with some of the other female guests in the capacious ladies bathroom, where the floor and walls were made from the same warm, creamy coloured marble, with antique brass fittings that were all polished to a high sheen.

"Ah! At last! There they are!" Jake said to Magda and Dave. "Beginin' to think we might 'ave to send out a search party for you!" he called out to Sophie and Mel as they came back into the huge room and walked hurriedly towards them.

Magda laughed, saying, "Many a true word is spoken in jest Jake! It does go on, and on in here! Some areas are like a labyrinth, *and that has happened!* But all the rooms the girls probably looked into now only lead off and then back into the same corridor, as we certainly could not have our guests keep getting lost on the way to and from the bathrooms!"

Sophie and Mel sat themselves down again apologising for being a long time, and then they immediately started telling their boyfriends all about the amazing décor in the many rooms they'd seen and briefly looked in, and about the amazing experiences the other girls and ladies were having with Magda's sisters that they had shared with them in the bathroom.

" 'Ere, Soph, now *I can get a word in...!*" Jake grinned at her. "...'old on a minute an' try this water Ruth brought!" He said when Sophie finally paused for breath, and he passed her a full glass from one of the small round tables at the side of the sofa.

"It's not like any water I've ever 'ad before!"

With an amused and quizzical look at him she took a sip. Her pale blue eyes lit up and she held the glass high and close to her face to look into it.

"Wow! That's – just water?! It tastes really...*Fresh!* Nothing like the tap water at home!" She said, and then drank most of it!

Magda said, "Yes, that is just water, but water *as it should be*...just pure natural water. Quite unlike the water you are supplied with at your homes by your town's authorities, the water you are drinking now doesn't have any of a long list of chemicals added into it that harm you. Amongst some of the most damaging chemicals on that list is flouride of course."

Dave had passed Mel her glass of water as well, and having drank some she more or less repeated what Sophie had just said, she then continued, "...a friend of mine at work, at the printers, she's really against flouride being put into the water, and in toothpaste, she told me a bit about how bad it is for you, so I, we, me and Dave, only drink bottled water now, and use non flouride toothpastes, but even that water isn't as anything like as nice as this..." and Dave said he totally agreed with her.

"That is very wise , as bottled water is much better for you than tap water, but even bottled water can be tampered with...there are several ways you can almost totally purify your water at home, it is a very good idea to do some research into it, and you will all be really helping yourselves by reducing, as much as you can, the input of all the dangerous poisons that play such havoc with your bodies, and your minds..."

Magda took a long drink as well, put her glass down, and

said, "So! We are approaching the last lap now for tonight! Then we can have a relax before you go. What we are talking about now brings me nicely round to what I want to continue with…

"So…Deep inside your brain, in fact right in the middle of it, between your left and right hemispheres, you have a small gland called 'the pineal gland', I mentioned it before when I was talking about your crown chakra. It is called that because it looks a little bit like a pine cone. This pineal gland is about the size of the end of your little finger, and it actually has within it rods and cones similar to those you have in your eyes, you could say that it is a third eye, an inner eye, your mind's eye…

"…It is that and much more. Technically it is a biological hyper-dimensional gateway, for you to reach and see into much higher levels of consciousness. When the pineal is working properly and has been fully awakened you can see into and explore other dimensions by astral travelling. 'Astra' means 'star', when you astral travel – which is an out of body experience, when your soul, your spirit, your consciousness, your ka - it has many names! - when it travels out into other dimensions and times, it remains connected to your physical body by what is called 'the silver cord'. This is an energy link, from your pineal gland to your travelling, non physical astral body...

"...However, please *do not ever attempt* to astral travel for the first few times without expert guidance, because there are negative elemental entities in the lower realms of the astral plane that will deceive and trick you, and they can cause havoc with your astral *and physical bodies and minds...*"

She paused, looking at the two couples, hoping that she wasn't overloading them too much with all of this esoteric information, even though she had done her best to present it all in as simplified and an introductory way as she could.

Mel then asked, "So...this...tiny 'pine cone, pineal gland'...in my brain, that I didn't even know was there...! It – it's so small and it - can do all that?! And I *think* I understand what you mean by *all that...*!"

Dave was quick to follow her saying, "That's incredible! I didn't know about it either! How come we're not taught about that at school?! I had no idea! Did you Jake – Sophie?" Neither of them had, they just shook their heads slowly.

Jake then said, "No mate, I 'aven't, I'm a bit gob-smacked, *even after everythin' else tonight...!*"

Magda, relieved that her intuition had been right – of course (!) - that they were ready to be presented with all this extra knowledge tonight - as Jake had put it - 'even after everythin' else tonight'. But one never knew, especially with a group, sometimes you could only go so far and then new information had to be presented very gradually, bit by bit, and over several meetings together. Sometimes though, as with this group, she'd immediately felt and sensed that each of them was more than awakened enough to be more than ready and capable of taking on the extra load of all this new information in just tonight's meeting.

"I'm so pleased..." She said quietly, "...So pleased that you are all – sorry! My thought's were wandering...! Let me answer you, Melanie and David...Yes! It can do all of that! Even though it is so small! - *It is one of those cases where size doesn't matter!*" She smiled at Mel.

"And David – you asked: 'why is it not taught in schools'?!" She raised one eyebrow, and smiled again, "you will recall what I was saying earlier about your schools and educational institutions? Well, this is another revealing example of their 'latent agenda' of course - that certainly doesn't want all the young developing minds becoming aware of this and other such things like your chakras, as all that would very soon lead them to start perceiving the full realisation of who and what they truly are - and are truly capable of! Because as soon as that happens their programming would break down, and then they would not be able to be controlled and manipulated so easily!

"So controlling and manipulating their *perception* to disconnect them from what is really possible for them, results then in them *believing* in only a very limited, and totally false or phantom version of reality – because that is what the system requires, and most often, with so many, tragically, it is successful, and so that is what they believe for the rest of their lives..."

Dave shook his head saying, "Oh Yes, of course...of course...! You're right...I wasn't thinking, just blurted it out, just..."

"- It is an important question, don't be hard on yourself...it is a question that anyone who cares about others would naturally ask! – and I know you all thought of it as well...?" They all nodded in silent agreement.

"You see, it is one of the main ways your...society...is manipulated, as any type of consciousness that is not directly related to the production and consumption of material goods is stigmatized, and it will therefore condemn and try to eradicate any other mentality and consciousness...

"Amongst the masses it only promotes and values left brain production-problem-solving, and devalues all other states of consciousness...because manipulating it so makes you humans ultimately create vast outpourings of negative energies, for the reasons Anders has explained...not the least of which by any means, is the making of humans into debt slaves as well due to the insidious doctrine of constant and excessive material consumption...As a relevant aside, Albert said, Albert Einstein, one of your recent great thinkers, is credited with saying, although in truth it was actually his first wife – Mileva – who said it first to him, but he said it publicly and so it is attributed to him:

'You cannot solve a problem with the same level of consciousness that created it...'

"Remember those words, and try to really *understand* them, they are so insightful and so important, and they will explain so much to you...Anders talked to you about the futility of 'protesting', 'shouting against' and 'fighting for...', *well, Mileva's words also help to explain why...*

"...But! – *Back to the pineal!* - You might be interested to know that in the Vatican, the biggest statue or sculpture there is of...a pine-cone! Indeed the whole place is riddled with that imagery and artifacts portraying it. It is also contained within the sacred geometry of the great cathedrals and churches. So too within all of the Eastern religions, and before they appeared, the old Egyptian mystery schools which stemmed from such knowledge as this that was known by far, far more ancient societies that were well aware of all this. The pine-cone pineal imagery is depicted amongst all of these in plain sight – so you have to ask yourself - 'Why? What is it about the pineal that they all knew...and know'...? - The answer of course is what you are now being introduced to, and starting to learn about. So...as Ander's might say: 'if you want to learn and to know more about all this specifically- there is a bit – or actually a lot more - Homework for you all'!"

She smiled at them, then reached down, picking up her glass from a shiny black and gold lacquered table to drink some more of the water.

"This water that Ruth kindly brought for us to drink has, as I have said, no flouride in it. Flouride is a poisonous and highly toxic chemical – a Doctor called Dean Burke, who, after spending over thirty years working and researching in the American National Cancer Institute, said about flouride:

'...In point of fact, flouride causes more human cancer death and causes it faster than any other chemical...'

"So Melanie, your friend at work was quite right in what she told you. Flouride has to be handled in secure containers, and those transporting them have to wear fully protective clothing and breathing apparatus – before they go and dump it into your drinking water...!

"Which is more than shocking when you realise that on a tube of toothpaste with flouride in it, it says: 'harmful if swallowed', and 'seek medical attention'! Yet strangely there are no such warnings on your kitchen taps!

"Incidentally it only takes *fifteen thousandths of a gram* per kilo of body weight to be lethal – to kill – an adult human. And only *five thousandths of a gram* per kilo to be lethal for a child....possibly even less now for children, because their young, fledgling immune systems are being so devastatingly damaged by all the toxic contents of the many vaccines they are deliberately forced to be injected with at such young ages.

"Flouride is also an industrial waste product that would be very expensive – costing thousands of dollars or pounds per truck load to dispose of it by the chemical industries because of its toxicity – Oh! There we are! An example for you of – 'production-problem-solving-consciousness'...that more than just borders on the psychopathic...!

"Amongst its other deadly attributes to humans, flouride severely damages the pineal gland, which is the prime purpose of getting humans to consume it. Sometimes it damages it *totally* irreparably, what it does is calcify or clog it up, so it can't function anything like it should do - if at all.

"Flouride was first used against humans back in the eighteen nineties with the appearance of teeth cleansing pastes. The Nazi's took its use much further in their concentration camps, before and during the Second World War...mainly on the recommendation to Himmler by Fritz Ter Meer, the chief executive officer of I.G. Farben, one of the biggest companies in the German chemical industries - chemical industries of which some are still household names today...

"Ter Meer only served three years in prison after the Nuremberg Trials as a war criminal, he then went straight into the chairman's job at Bayer A.G., a huge German pharmaceutical company, in nineteen fifty one. He, they, knew of course that flouride was also very effective in making people, the prisoners, much more docile, dumbed down, and compliant labour slaves...

"There was as well, the added benefit of speeding up their demise – killing them - in a very cost effective manner...as they were always being replaced with new, fresh batches of prisoner-slaves...

"Stalin, one of the 'greatest' mass murdering psychopaths of the last century, *amongst many others*, realised that he could reduce the number of guards needed in each of the many Gulag prison camps by at least two thirds - if concentrated flouride was put in the prisoner-slaves drinking water, because of its effect in dociling them...

"And so, as you become aware of all this, any sane, normal person would have to ask: 'so why is it *still* being 'allowed' to be used...*against all of us...?'* Well...the mendacious replies from those promoting the 'manifest agenda' are: - *'Oh but it's good for you!'* - *'Because it helps prevent tooth decay...! We are only trying to help you...! - Because we care so much about your teeth!'* But the real reason is hidden within the malefic latent agenda that I have just briefly explained.

"Incidentally – the tooth decay prevention argument they lie to you about – and please do research all this for yourselves – and you will quickly discover that it is a very well crafted fallacy, and so the people have been well and truly fooled of course – you recall Samuel's - Mark 's words..?...

"Actually you can much more effectively help to prevent tooth decay by regularly brushing them with sodium bicarbonate – 'baking soda' - which alkalises or neutralises, the acids produced from foods, particularly from the deliberately harmful manufactured foods which attack tooth enamel, because it helps to neutralise the dangerously excessive amounts of poisonous refined sugar acidity that is put into all of them. As it is ingested in your bodies, just one of the many detrimental things this type of sugar does to you is help to form powerfully corrosive acids - and the more acidic your bodies become the more prone they are to obesity, diabetes and a host of other serious and degenerative diseases. The opposite of the word 'acidic' is 'alkaline', and the more alkaline the body's chemical balance is the healthier it generally is.

"Oh...just as a final comment on refined sugar consumption – in seventeen hundred an individual's average consumption was around only four pounds in weight *a year* – and that was only by those whom could afford to buy it, and they were in a minority!   But by the year two thousand and eight it was around *one hundred and eighty pounds a year* 'by everybody'! – That is very nearly thirteen stones! – Probably about what you weigh David!   And that is *annually* for an average North American!   So over ten years that is nearly a ton of it going into each of their bodies!   *Does anyone really think that consuming all that refined sugar and its attendant acidity is beneficial to a human body and mind...?!*

"The only things that are 'healthy' about it are the financial profits gleaned by those companies whom sell it...and the profits of their corporate allies in the pharmaceutical industries which run into the billions of dollars and pounds in profits from selling their treatments for all of the illnesses it causes! And of course, underlying it all, the 'healthy' furtherance - *of the parasites' agenda..."*

Jake, along with the others, looked absolutely shocked at these pronouncements from Magda.

"Crikey me!   That's a bloomin' crazy amount o' sugar! I know we in England might be eatin' a bit less of it *– but prob'ly not by much!* I, for one, am definitely goin' to watch and limit 'ow much I'm 'avin' from now on!"

"Me too!" The others all said together.

"I'm definitely going to do some research into all this - *and overhaul my diet!"* Sophie said.

"Magda smiled at her saying,"...well done, good decision! When you research all this you will also discover some foods – and all foods are basically just forms of energy that your bodies need by converting them into usable energy – that are beneficial and effective to cleanse and help activate your pineal gland – and you will also discover the long listing of those that do not. Most of those are deliberately placed on your supermarkets' shelves to be within easy reach...

"Food is a huge subject that we will talk about another day. Before we do that the research you will hopefully start to do now will prime you for that next time, and as a result of your research you will become more and more aware, that like your water, your manufactured foods contain many, many deliberately added poisons as well...so forearmed with that knowledge you can start and try to avoid them, by eating only natural, good, healthier produced foods.

"But! - Here's some good news for you! You will all be pleased to know, as examples of those good foods, those 'good usable energies' - that raw cacao and dark chocolate really help to decalcify your pineal!"

"I knew it!" Jake exclaimed loudly! *"I knew that chocolate cake was good for you! - Bloomin' glad I don't 'ave to give that up!"*

"Well it's a good job it is...!" Sophie said, loudly laughing with everyone else, "...*As you eat enough of it...!*"

"Er, I shall ignore that comment from the cheap shot seats..." Jake replied with mock chagrin, his voice sounding just like The Beatle, John Lennon!

Smiling, Magda said, "Yes, I agree – but only about the chocolate cake that Alfie serves in 'The Trocadero', as his wife bakes everything there with only the purest, poison free of ingredients, unlike those your 'cake factories' use!"

"Aye! She must do! I thought it was about the best I'd ever 'ad! Just wish now though...that I 'adn't 'ad...*quite so much...!*" He said, rubbing his stomach. Sophie put a hand over her mouth to hide her grinning at him.

Putting her glass down onto the small table, Magda continued, "Now, perhaps, you can start – to see – pun intended! How...with some training and much practice you have all the means and the ability to see...auras?!"

247

Jake said to her, his jocular tone now replaced with a more serious one, "yeah, I think I am...y're sayin' that...a bit like an engine...that if all the parts in it are workin' as they should do it'll motor along nicely, and get y'to where y'want to go to...but if a small part...in the electrics say, in't workin' when it should, or not at all, then the engine might get y'so far, for a while, but it just in't gonna get y'all the way there...so y'waste y'time bein' distracted by tinkerin' with it, so y'eventually give up or forget about that journey y'wanted to go on...er, if that makes any sense...?!"

"Yes Jake, I would say that makes a lot of sense. Because what you have just done is take on board all the new information I've presented, and then approached it, to try to process and understand it, in a way that currently makes sense to you by comparing it with something you already know, or are, at least, more familiar with. But far more importantly you have *approached it with an open mind*, not one constrained or limited by the programmed ingrained scepticism that is encouraged by 'the system' to be used by most humans. *So well done you!*"

"Oh! Ta! Huh! Well – Looks like I'm gonna 'ave to recognize it - *an' embrace it now then...!*" He said, his jocular tone back again.

Sophie looked at him with an amused and expectant expression, expecting a follow up joke or funny comment.

Jake looked at her and said, "'Ey! *No I'm serious!...*Said before that I've just spent at least three days an' 'alf twice strippin' down an engine that *should work* – that's why I 'ad to get away from it today, before I pulled all me hair out, an' I then 'ad a feelin' to go down t' harbour this dinnertime for some fresh air, clear me head from it for a bit. An' that's when I saw you sat there Soph'...an' if I 'adn't I wouldn't be 'ere now...! I reckon I need to double check them brand new little electrical parts I fitted, just assumed they were all workin', them bein' new ones like! Bet it's one o' them playin' up! Bloomin' 'eck! That's it! *So it's one o' those coincidences – that aren't coincidences innit!* The answer has cum to me! Or...I made it...cum to me! Awesome!...Sorted it! - I 'ope! *Thanks Magda!*"

"Oh don't thank me Jake! As you said, 'you made it come to you!', you desired, then you created – and then you recognized it when 'the answer' came to you!" She laughed.

Jake sat back immensely satisfied, and Sophie squeezed and rubbed his shoulder, pleased for him.

"Now, moving on..." Magda said, "if you all just raise a hand, either one, in front of you like this..." She held her right hand up with the palm facing her, fingers straight and spread apart, their tips at eye level about a foot or so away from her face.

"Try and position yourself so that as you look at your hand, in the background there is nothing to distract you, the walls are ideal." They all shuffled themselves around to do that.

"Now, make sure you are really comfy, and you are not having to strain to keep your hand up, lower it a bit if you need to...good, now stare at your fingertips, keep your eyes still, let them even go out of focus a little...take deep slow breaths in through your nose...and slowly out of your mouth...and focus on your breathing to help limit your mind wandering with random thoughts, and really concentrate your gaze on and around your finger tips..."

Her voice had got quieter and quieter as she spoke, until she was silent. She watched them all as they followed her instructions, and after a few minutes she said, "Aaaand relax...!"

Everyone lowered their hands, closing and opening their eyes as they refocused on their surroundings. "What did you see?" Magda quietly asked them.

"I think I saw a bit of thin whitish blurring round my hand." Dave said. "But I don't know if that was, well, just my eyes going funny as I stared?!"

"Mmm, so did I, it came and went though, but at the end it - that blurryness - sort of got a bit thicker, just a bit.." Mel said.

"Yeah, that's what I sort of saw as well, bit like a thinnish misty glove..." Sophie said. "But it was best when I sort of didn't look right at it, but a bit to one side, like at night if you look to the side of or a bit above a star, you can then see it better!"

"I saw sort o' blurry pale colours not just white ones though, I think!" Jake said.

"Excellent! Well done!" Magda said. "For your first attempt that was a success! As you practice more and more, and reduce all the poisons in your diets that disrupt and sabotage your abilities, it is like anything else, the better you will be able to do it. And you will – I was going to say 'sub-consciously' but actually it is 'higher-consciously', see, by using more than just your two eyes...

"...And, as I said to you Jake, approaching these ability exercises 'with an open and non-sceptical mind' is so important. As you refine your own individual techniques, by practising on yourselves, when you look at others, especially at the head and shoulders region, eventually you will be able to, and ever increasingly so – see their auras all around them. Also not just the blurry white auras you started to see just now but gradually as your ability increases you will start to see their colour shades – interestingly Jake you said you already saw a pale pastel colour as well?"

"Yeah, I think I did. Think it was a bit, er, like pale purpley in the whitey blur, kept cumin' an' goin' tho'..."

"You remember when I closed in on the rainbow earlier...? When the colours all faded into blurry shades? Then, when I opened it out again you could see all the bright colours? Well, that is similar to what is happening now. At the moment you are just glimpsing shades of what is there, and in time, with practice, and changes to the type of foods you eat and the water you drink, it is possible that you will see the vibrancy of the full colours, and just how far – which is many, many feet from most people – they really do extend.

"I could talk to you about the many aspects of this phenomena all night! But for now I'll just mention a few things about it as examples – of the effects that other peoples' emotional auras have on you, and yours on theirs!

"So...with some people you can have an immediate feeling of...pleasantry, you feel at ease with them – but with others it can be quite the opposite. Well, when all that happens, you are sensing and interacting with their auras, your higher awareness is automatically decoding their auric – from the word aura - energy frequencies, which emanate from their emotional frequencies.

"You can also, it is quite easy to do, consciously draw your aura much closer in to you, so it doesn't interact randomly with others – especially useful in a crowd! – Or when you go to a busy town centre on a shopping trip for example! You know how draining that experience can be sometimes! Well yes, there is physical tiredness from the effort of walking and carrying bags full of shopping, but the real reason is the constant interacting with so many random, and often, perhaps, more negatively skewed auras...

"But! Another time when we meet I will go into more detail about all of this for you! For today, it was important to take the first step and just introduce and guide you to the basics, so you can proceed to develop them by researching and practising on your own now…I just need to give you some final, everyday practical advice on when to use them, for now."

Sophie asked: "So when Anders was saying before that we already have within us, the abilities to, well, to protect ourselves – with what you have shown us – focusing on our chakras then creating the diamond, and starting to see peoples' auras, that is what he meant, and what we have to do?"

"Essentially…in essence – yes." Magda replied. "I'm not saying you have to be walking around in every moment of every day trying to see *every body's* aura all of the time at this stage! Eventually as you advance with this you will be able to switch from your normal sight to your 'extra-normal' sight in an instant and then back again at will, but that will take time and practice. It will be, with practise, just the same with your protective diamonds - as and when you feel you need to summon it, it will be in place in, in more or less, an instant…

"But I would suggest that from now on whenever you get even the merest feeling, sensing, or even the slightest intuitive inkling, that one, or more of the Watchers or Wreckers maybe in your proximity - *fully trust those feelings!* Because the more you trust and believe in them and use them – and use them for everything not just in this extreme case - they will respond just like the physical muscles in your bodies do – the more they are used the stronger they will become! - They are your natural 'hyper-awarenesses muscles', and they are a vital part of your natural defences and discernment as well...!

"...So, if and when you sense their presence, what I suggest is that you then immediately summon your protective diamond, then use your extra-normal sight, to carefully, and discreetly look around you to identify where it, or they are. Actually, just let me go off on a slight tangent to that for a minute...

"Developing your normal peripheral vision to discretely see and notice things around you is a very useful skill to acquire as well. Highly adept martial artists can do this, and Intelligence Agencies train their covert field operatives to walk down a street just staring straight ahead, but by using and developing their peripheral vision they can be trained to read the house numbers, or later accurately describe the appearances of people that were at either side of them, try doing it yourself. As you gain the skill you will be amazed at how much more you can see and observe all around you! Most people only see, focus on and observe a very limited area that is directly in front of them.

"So...going back - however you do it, do so ideally without them realising you are looking for them, or that you have seen them, then remember what they look like, and get yourself away from them as soon as you can - without alerting them to the fact they've been spotted by you! Then, as soon as you can, alert the others in your group, describing the appearance of who or what you saw to them, so they can be on their guard as well. Hopefully the 'group' of awakening people you know will be growing all the time, nurtured to grow by each of you as you all talk and communicate with each other. So for those others of you who may be in the vicinity being forewarned will be forearmed.

"We are concerned that more Watchers and more Wreckers are being recruited, but that won't happen overnight. As their legions grow though more and more will be deployed everywhere as they attempt to, to quash the masses from this new awakening of humanity."

Dave, like the others, was engrossed in what Magda was saying, and a thought came to him that he wanted to ask Magda's opinion about, "Er, earlier, in 'The Trocadero', Anders said that awakened people's auras are bigger and brighter, than those, those of peoples that aren't....so they can be spotted and seen easier, and the Watchers' and Wreckers' were like dark shadowy overlays - Mel asked him if it was like *'moths to a flame'*, so...you've said that we can pull in or draw in our auras to make them smaller – so would it be useful if we did that as well? I mean if it's smaller – like a smaller flame, it can't be seen as easily… can it? Is that a good idea as well...?!"

"Yes, it is a good idea, and well thought of David!" Magda replied. "But...I think Jake can answer that for you by me asking him a different question first!"

Jake quickly sat up, aware that he was suddenly the focus of everyone's attention.

"Oh! Er, yeah 'course, well I'll try like! – *Er...s'long as it's not too 'ard a one!"* He chuckled.

"Not at all! Even if it was I'm sure you would work out an answer to it anyway! What I want to ask you Jake, is this: do you remember what happened the first time you tried to ride a motorbike…?"

"Ah! *Aye! - That one's easy enough!* I do! Hah! *Er, bit embarrasin' it were!* Nearly ran into a parked car! – Panicked, locked the brakes, skidded - and then fell off it! Still got a scar on me knee from that!" He laughed. "Took me a long time to get the 'ang of everything I 'ad to do to balance an' stay on it, move it, use the gears an' clutch, the brakes an' indicators, slow it and stop it – usin' different hands an' feet for it all, and that were in a big car park – and then, when I eventually went on't road with it – *nightmare!* Everythin' else were movin' around me an' at me as well! - Took a good while to get the 'ang of it an' learn do it all properly, an' safely, y'just gotta keep practisin'…*AH! An' I know now why y'asked me that Magda!*"

"I knew you would Jake! But, now, these days, would you say you just get on your motorbike, and ride it without consciously thinking about all of the many essential things that different parts of your body have to do, and you do them all rapidly and in complete synchrony?"

"Oh yeah! It's just natural now, the bike sort o' just becomes part o' me like…!"

"So David, does that help to answer you?"

"Yes it does!...Of course, *brilliant way to answer it!* - You did say you were showing us, introducing us, to just the basics...So yeah, sort of, well, learn it one-step-at-a-time until it becomes 'natural, and part of you', like Jake said – that's what you're saying?!"

"That's right! These are new abilities and skill sets for you all to learn, so it is always best to thoroughly learn all about the basics before adding and refining your techniques, and everyone learns and becomes able to do all of this at different rates.

"There are three stages to *any* skill acquisition, the first stage is called the 'Cognitive phase', this is when you have to consciously and deliberately think about every individual action before you attempt it. The second phase is the 'Associative phase', where there is less deliberate thinking as you become more accustomed to what you have to do. The final stage is the 'Autonomous phase', when all the response actions happen automatically. Top performers involved in sporting activities talk about *'spontaneous movement that supersedes conscious thought'*, for example. "

Magda then stood up, saying that she was just going over to have a word with Ruth as it was nearly time for them all to return to the Fair, and that perhaps a few minutes to talk amongst themselves might be a welcome break from constantly listening to her voice!

They watched her walking away for a moment and then they all began talking to each other at once, bouncing their thoughts around, discussing and jumping from topic to topic that had been revealed to them that evening.

Sophie was thoroughly enjoying herself, and especially so having Jake here sharing and being involved with her in all of this, it just felt really good, and her, their, new friends were such nice people, and so much on the same wavelength as well. She sat back for a moment just to muse on how this amazing day for her had panned out since she had first sat at her desk in the office this morning – that seemed a lot longer back though than only this morning! So much had happened! - She'd then been sitting on the bench at the harbour and Jake had just appeared to her - then sitting back at the office - then sitting on the bike - then sitting on the unicorn at the merry-go-round - then sitting in The Trocadero – and then sitting here! Gosh! What a lot of sitting I've done on different things and in different – *very different* places today! She thought. All that sitting down *and I'm absolutely tired out now!* I'll sleep like a log tonight, and she tried to stifle a yawn but it turned into fully blown one with both her hands over her mouth!

"Oh...I'm sorry! I've just come over – (yawn again) – all tired all of a sudden!"

"Oh don't – you'll – (yawn) – set me off too...!" Mel said, yawning now as well.

"You alright Soph'?" Jake asked her.

"Yeah thanks, I've just come over – (yawn) – sorry! A bit tired! It's been an amazing day! And I didn't get much sleep last night either thinking about – (yawn) - *everything I'd heard from Anders last night!*"

"Well you just nod off if y'want! - But don't y'start snorin' as we're in company. – *Might not get invited back!*" He whispered his last words loudly and humorously to her, then looked over to Dave and Mel, slightly shaking his head when he said to them with his deadpan humour, "Eeh, I dunno!...*Can't tek 'er anywhere..!*"

She poked his arm and sat up again, saying, "Huh! *I don't snore!* And even if I did they'd just be quiet lady-like ones!" She giggled. "But anyway, I'm fine now – I just needed to have a few good yawns!"

Jake was about to put his arm around her when his whole body suddenly shuddered, his chest expanded, he arched his back, and shaking his head, mouth wide open, he let out a gargantuan groaning yawn!

He sounds just like a big old grizzly bear! she thought! "Wow! - *Foghorn you!*" She then said to him her eyes wide in amused surprise. "Thought you were going to have a fit! Look! You've set Dave and Mel off again!"

Amongst all their yawnings they hadn't noticed that Magda had returned and was looking at them with great amusement, and she said, "Oh, dear! *This must be the sleepy corner!* We must have tired you all out!"

She sat back down with them, waving her hands dismissively as they all politely apologised.

"No don't apologise at all! I'm not surprised! You've all had so much to absorb I'm not in the least surprised!...I'm only sorry to have to tell you that you might all have a bit of 'jet-lag' as well tomorrow because when you go back to the Fair in a few minutes, it will be about the same time as when you left it!"

Sophie looked at her watch. "Oh wow! It's well after midnight! She exclaimed. The others expressed the same amazement, as the time had seemed to just fly by.

"When you are back in the caravan you will need to wind back your watches – because the time there will be what it was when you entered 'The Trocadero'!" Magda said. "Before we go, and you are the last to leave as you can see, everyone else has left already..."

They leaned over the sofas to look out from the cosy alcove that had partially cocooned them from the rest of the room and saw that they were indeed the last of the guests. Magda's sisters were nowhere in sight either.

"...I must say that it is not very often that I have the opportunity to talk for so long and about *quite so much* all in one visit with a group of first time guests! But I just knew you were all ready and able to take it all in!" Magda said.

"So I thought it was appropriate to reveal, and awaken you to a lot more of the very important facts that you needed to know, now, and I hope that I managed to achieve some of that. As well of course to explain and show you how to start to protect yourselves, which is what Anders specifically asked us to do for you.

"Hopefully then, our meeting tonight has further fuelled your desire to do more research on your own and together. Such research will lead you on to discover many things that you will find exciting, but sometimes confusing, and sometimes dismaying...but we can all look forward to sharing those together, and moving ever upwards with them when we meet next time.

"Knowledge - coupled with Understanding - *Is Power!* - But it is only the *application* of Knowledge and Understanding, and their resulting Power, that can change anything."

She reached down for her nearly empty glass of water, and held it up in front of her.

"This glass only has a small amount of water in it now as you can see. If I were to quickly pour a lot more water into it from high up above it, all the water would surge, splash and churn around in some turmoil, but it would soon settle again, and the water level, after it had settled, would of course be much higher up the glass.

"It is a good example of how, when new, fresh knowledge is added to the vessel – to a vessel that is open and able to receive it, at first it causes some turmoil, but it soon adjusts to the new, higher level, and settles again, until more is added.

"Earlier, I said to myself *'I was so pleased'*, and *'sorry - my thoughts had been wandering'*, what I was thinking then and what I meant was that I was, I am, *so pleased for you all!* Yes, no doubt there has been some turmoil within you all tonight – and most likely there still is, as all this new knowledge has just been poured in so quickly...But you are all 'settling' so very well! And so very quickly and now your 'levels' are so much higher up! It is not often, as I have said, that I add quite so much in one go to 'vessels', shall we say, as I have done tonight...! But I sensed that you all have awakened so much that...I...felt duty bound to...you were more than ready...so well done to you all...*and it has been a delight for me to meet you...*

"...All I, all we, have done is reveal and guide you towards

267

some of the many paths that you can now choose to take you...somewhere, literally, *wonder-full*...that you were always meant to be going towards...!...*So, once again, I say that it has been a delight for me to meet you all...and I thank you.*"

At that she stood up, her hands by her sides, she was a picture of pure benign humility. Her warm smile and the loving light from her bright green eyes radiated out from her, caressing over them all.

Sophie and Mel looked up at her, and both of them burst into tears.

Jake and Dave had to blink rapidly, their eyes moistening, and they took deep breaths to steady their emotions. Mel, sitting the nearest to Magda shot up and gave her a long hug, sniffling her thanks to her, and Sophie quickly followed her to do the same.

Jake and Dave were now standing as well, hugging their loved ones close to them as the girls had rushed back into their arms after hugging Magda.

"Oh, oh I'm so sorry! - *But I'm So Happy!*" Sophie sniffled as she wiped her eyes and looked up into Jakes face.

"Heyyy, *don't be sorry!*...I'm 'appy too, an' to be 'onest – I, I feel like doin' the same meself..." He said quietly to her, gently hugging her close again. After a moment he took a deep breath and reached out his long arm to shake Magda's hand.

"*Well!* I must say I really thought it might be 'in the cards' for me to have nice big hugs from two handsome young men tonight!" Magda said with a laugh and a mischievous teasing glint in her eyes, her hands on her hips.

With a laugh Jake gently unfurled himself from Sophie and went to Magda and stooped down to give her a big hug, Dave then did the same. They all then started to walk slowly together, across the now empty room over to the door, to leave.

"*Magda, how...er,* when or where, and how...*will we meet you again...will...?*" Sophie asked her.

"Oh do not worry about that my dear, either I or one of my

sisters – probably Ruth, as you have already met her, will come regularly now to you. To you all. And you will all visit here many more times. Perhaps next time Jake can visit the library – all of you can – and Dave will be interested to see our art galleries – as I am sure you all will be too!"

As Magda got to the portal door, she turned to address them all and said, "I, we, are now connected to you, so if at any time, you really, really need to see me, or if you need our help, for any reason, just reach out with your thoughts, and, in the words of one of your popular songs:

'Just Think Of Me! – *And I'll Be There...*!'"

The two girls' tears flowed again. And then they all followed Magda out through the doorway next to the one they had earlier come in through.

They emerged in the interior of the Romany caravan which was a bit crowded with them all now standing in it. They looked around at the space saving fittings and layout that had all the essentials to cosily live in it.

"Wow, this is lovely Magda!" Sophie said, wiping her eyes. Jake was looking around and admiring all the intricate woodwork, and the delicate carvings in it.

"Aye – it is, it's brilliant!" He said. "An' everythin' looks to be 'andmade – whoever made all o' this certainly knew what they were doin'!"

"Thank you! It was made a long, long time ago for me by a master craftsman, it is my little home sometimes when I am travelling *on*...here, and I love it dearly." Magda replied, running her hand over some of the darkly polished woodwork that shone with the deep patina of age.

"I love it too!" Mel said. "I'd much rather live in something like this Dave - than our damp little flat!"

"D'y'know – so would I!" He said with enthusiasm.

Magda laughed, and said, "Well, you never know! That might be something else for you to think about as well!"

271

"Oh! - Is that the time now – *'here'* - Magda?" Dave asked her, looking at the round clock-face of an antique looking time piece on the wall, the ornate hands of which were showing the time to be just after eight thirty in the evening!

"Yes, I'm afraid it is! I hope that you all won't be too tired tomorrow with a few hours less sleep, as your bodies will think it is now getting on for one o'clock in the morning!" Magda replied.

"Ah no problem! I'll catch up on me beauty sleep sometime! But I think an early night - *after some fish n' chips wi' mushy peas tho'* might be a good idea, don't you Soph'?" Jake said.

"Now that sounds like a plan! *I'm starving now!*" She said, then turned to Mel and Dave.

"Do you want to come back to my house with us, there's a chip shop just round the corner, I can ring up and order before we set off, and we'll pick them up?!"

"Oh that sounds good! - D'you think so Mel…?"

"Oooh! Yes! *Fish n' chips!* - If you're sure that's alright with you Sophie?"

"'Course! Great! Let's do it!"

After more hugs and more tears as they said their goodbyes, for now, to Magda, with the promise of meeting her again soon, first Sophie and Jake, then a few minutes later, Mel and Dave left Magda's Romany caravan. They all met up again just beyond the caravan, and walked together back through the busy Fair towards the car park field.

Suddenly being amongst so many people – and such a medley of noises and coloured lights - back in the 'real world' again, seemed very strange to them at first.

They slowly made their way through all the people coming and going and Sophie made her phone call to the chip shop with their orders, and gave directions to Dave and Mel to where she lived. As they walked Jake kept his watchful eyes out on the people around them, trying to use his peripheral vision as well like Magda had suggested...They soon arrived at the exit into the car park field, and just as Dave and Mel were about to separate from them to go to their car, Sophie looked back at the Fair – and saw Ruth - dressed quite differently now though in jeans and a blue hoodie sweatshirt, discreetly waving goodbye to them with a big smile on her face. She must have followed us, she thought.

"Look there's Ruth! She's waving..!" She called to the others who all turned and waved back, some people then walked in front of Ruth for a moment, and when they had moved away she was no longer there.

Back at the bike Jake carefully took their helmets out of the shoulder bag, handed Sophie hers, then he held up high the colourful glass vase, and it caught within it the glowing light from the setting sun and reflected back sparkling rainbows of colours onto them both.

As he stared at it he said, in a quiet, awe struck voice, as he suddenly realised something, "d'y'know Soph' – I think...it's gotta be a sort o', well, our good luck memento o' this amazin' evenin' - *'cause if it adn't been for this 'ere vase needin' to go in me bag before we went on that merry-go-round..."*

"I know...I'm going to treasure it forever...*it's the best present I've ever had...thank you...*"

He smiled, looking deeply into her once more teary eyes, and kissed her tears away...gave her a long loving hug, and then harrumphed as he cleared his throat, and with a croaky but loud voice said to her,

"*C'mon then! Let's go! Fish n' chips!...An' everythin' else...Awaits Us...!*"

To be continued…!

Book 2 of the: 'It Awaits Us', saga is called:

'The Pandora Quest'

The author – is a *first-time* one! – But a *long-time* artist! He has a website of some of his artworks, you can see them, and contact him at:

www.fineartandfurnishings.co.uk

Made in the USA
Columbia, SC
16 May 2021